**Praise for
Shirley Hailstock**

YOU MADE ME LOVE YOU

"Hailstock pens a strong, moving drama. Tension fills nearly every page . . . pacing is fast, and the intrigue and danger are just as intense as the love that develops . . ."
—*Romantic Times*

"Ms. Hailstock always comes through with good details, plotting and a sense of adventure."—*Affaire de Coeur*

HIS 1-800 WIFE
(Selected by the Black Expressions Book Club)

"Shirley Hailstock is an exceptional writer. This is a departure from her usual romantic suspense novels but it is an incredibly successful one."—*Romantic Times*

"This book really took me by surprise. While Ms. Hailstock's last book [*More Than Gold*] was full of danger and intrigue, this one is a very up-close-and-personal. I love the journey her characters take as they realize and examine their mutual love for each other. A very moving story by an accomplished author."—*Old Book Barn Gazette*

WHISPERS OF LOVE
(Winner of the HOLT Medallion)

"[Ms. Hailstock's] . . . plots are over the top of the world."—*New York Times*

penseful. What more could you want?"—*Suzanne Forster*, Author of *Angel Face*

"*Legacy* is a riveting drama that blends the best elements of romance and suspense to create a quality literary liqueur too smooth and too lush not to be addictive!" —*Romantic Times Magazine*

WHITE DIAMONDS
(*Glamour magazine* "Fall in Love Again" List)

"*White Diamonds* is a fast-paced romantic suspense that entices readers to finish in one sitting. . . . The audience will shout "Hail, Hail," to Shirley Hailstock for a great story."—*Affaire de Coeur*

"Gripping. A powerful drama—a powerful love story." —*Stella Cameron* Author of *Glass Houses*

"Shirley Hailstock has once again raised the ordinary to extraordinary, the sublime to exquisite and bathed it in an exotic romantic fantasy."—*Romantic Times*

OPPOSITES ATTRACT
(National Readers Choice Award Finalist)

". . . Hailstock thoroughly explores the emotional conflicts of her characters . . ."—*Publishers Weekly*

"*Opposites Attract* is a complex, emotional love story with ribbons of poignancy pulling the romance together in a treat that is just too good to resist.—*Romantic Times*

"What are you thinking?" Owen asked as they rode up in the elevator.

"I can't tell you." Her head was on his shoulder and she leaned back, smiling up at him. He gazed at her for a moment, then dropped his mouth to meet hers.

"Are they good thoughts?" he muttered against her lips.

"The best." Stephanie held onto the end of the word, sliding her arm up his chest and moving around to fit herself into his body. It was prom night, graduation, her first date, all rolled into one.

"I want to know what they are."

"What?" Stephanie had forgotten his question.

Owen was looking at her, staring, openly fixated on her, as if he needed to commit her to memory.

Stephanie found the buttons on his shirt. With nervous fingers she pushed them through one by one until she could bury her hands against his heated skin. It was moist and warm and felt like velvet. She leaned forward and kissed his chest, feeling his rapidly beating heart against her tongue. Owen's hands threaded through her hair, pulling it free and allowing it to flow over her shoulders. He pulled her head back, keeping her mouth from tantalizing his nipples and looked deep into her eyes.

"That feels so good," he said.

The Secret

SHIRLEY HAILSTOCK

Dafina
Books

KENSINGTON PUBLISHING CORP.
http://www.kensingtonbooks.com

Acknowledgments

To the wonderful PATH (Parents As Tender Healers) trainers of adoptive and foster parents at Metro Select Arc in Avenel, New Jersey. They provided me with an eye-opening experience regarding the plight of so many children in our society. These unsung heroes and heroines who work daily to prepare willing parents for the children they accept in their homes. Thank you, not only for my own education for the child I am adopting, but for the insight into the need for additional loving families.

Prologue

Stephanie Hunter's calf muscles tightened as she went up on her tiptoes. Keeping her heels from clicking on the parquet flooring, she slipped into the back of the church. Fear and perspiration heated her skin despite the central air-conditioning. She swallowed, clamping down her rising heartbeat. Stephanie had no invitation and irrationally expected the entire congregation to turn and stare at her for crashing a wedding. Only a single man standing near the back nodded appreciatively at her arrival. She smiled back and took the offered arm of the groomsman who walked toward her.

First Baptist was an old church, seasoned with stained-glass windows and lemon polished pews. The faint aroma of the oil and the soft strands of organ music took Stephanie back to her childhood. The sanctuary was crowded. She listened to the hushed whisper of respectful voices as they waited for the wedding to commence.

"Bride or groom?" the man asked. It didn't matter to her which side she sat on. She didn't personally know either the bride or the groom.

"Groom," she said decisively. At least her connection to Bradley Clayton was greater than to his intended wife. He was her brother, well almost-brother.

The church was beautifully dressed for a July wedding. Flowers perfumed the air. Pecan wood and light filtering through the cathedral-style windows gave the room a warm glow that made Stephanie wish the couple good luck in their future together. As the music rose, the guests continued to arrive and like a practiced dance, the tuxedo-clad groomsmen ferried them to their seats. Stephanie trained her gaze on the groom and his best man standing under the high arching sanctum. Dr. Bradley Clayton, formerly of Dallas, now residing in Philadelphia, was nervously fingering his cuffs. He was good-looking. Very good-looking. In fact, he was gorgeous. The white tuxedo set off his dark skin enough that every woman in the audience would surely envy . . . she checked her program . . . Dr. Mallory Russell.

Two doctors, she thought. Dinner at their house would be in-depth discussions of operations and anatomy, something Stephanie's nervous stomach couldn't take. Next to Bradley stood another Clayton, Owen. He was equal to Bradley in looks. Taller by a couple of inches, with shoulders a football player would envy. Yet he didn't have a football player's build. He was tall and thin, his tuxedo fitting him as if it had been made for his body.

She admired the cut of it, thinking Owen Clayton could be a country gentleman in some costume drama, a businessman, or a beach bum and look equally at home. His hands were clasped together in front of him, but Stephanie thought he was hiding the fact that he was as nervous as his brother. Stephanie's gaze rested on Owen for a long appraising moment. He wasn't looking at her, yet her heart made a connection with him as it began to pound harder. Despite the nervousness and stress that weddings bring, Owen exuded a silent assurance, a confidence that would make him stand out no matter where he was. She'd never seen either man in person before today, but they were linked to her. And there were others.

Heads bobbed in front of her as a change in the music signaled the start of the processional. She looked around as groomsmen led two women down the aisle. One was in a wheelchair. The other walked. Mothers of the bride and groom, Stephanie thought and stretched her neck to see over the head bobbing and weaving in front of her. Which one was Devon Clayton?

Which one was her mother?

The bridesmaids and groomsmen started down the aisle. Stephanie matched up the names on her program with the faces that passed before her.

She'd scanned her own face in countless mirrors since she'd discovered her real identity. Today she wondered if she would see any resemblance of it in those who passed her on the way to the altar. Dean Clayton, a filmmaker. She'd found his photo on the Internet. He was younger than she by many years, a clean-cut, good-looking young man who could pose for the all-American boy poster. He had a bright smile and held the arm of his sister, model Rosa Clayton. Stephanie could turn a head if she wanted to, but she was nowhere near as model-beautiful as Rosa Clayton. Rosa elegantly glided down the aisle to the tune of *I Believe I Can Fly*. Stephanie hummed it softly, thinking what a beautiful song to begin a life together. A pang of jealousy went through her. It was unfair, she thought. Then she reminded herself that life was often unfair and these people had not cast her fate. That had been done by someone else, someone she had loved, would always love.

Mark and Luanne Rogers came next. She didn't know who they were, but they had to be close friends to be included in a wedding party primarily comprised of Claytons. The last of the Claytons was James. Another gorgeous specimen. He ran a carpentry business and had married two years earlier. She'd heard one of the other groomsmen call him Digger. She supposed, for a carpenter, it was an appropriate moniker. The entire group, spread like a posed photograph across the front of the church, looked at the congregation, awaiting the bride. They were a beautiful family, tall, proud, happy. Stephanie was proud she could claim a small part in it as her own.

The strains of the wedding march cut through the hush of movement. Heads turned as the congregation stood and the back doors, which had been momentarily closed, opened with a flourish. Standing there in a white lace gown was the bride. Mallory Russell's face, uncovered by a veil, shone with an inner glow that made her smile seem like a bright beam. A long white carpet was unrolled before her and a little girl of six or seven years dropped rose petals along it to the altar. The bride began a slow walk toward her groom. She was alone, smiling, holding her bouquet at waist level, but without anyone to give her away. A flash of empathy went through Stephanie's mind. She wondered what had happened in Mallory Russell's life that robbed her of a father or brother to escort her into the next phase of it. But Mallory's expression disclosed no regret. Her attention was on the man waiting for her in the front of the church.

Stephanie envied her.

"She's beautiful," someone next to her whispered. Stephanie took her eyes off the bride to look at the woman who spoke.

"She is," Stephanie said, surprised to find tears in her voice that had nothing to do with the ceremony. They were such a wonderful-looking family. Were they really hers? After all these years had she finally found the place where she belonged?

The wind snatched at her curly braids as Stephanie drove fast through the Dallas traffic. She wove in and out of lanes, around trucks and cars, easing the speedometer of her red convertible past eighty. She knew going to the reception was dangerous. Her plan had been to attend the wedding, watch from the background, unobserved. But plans change, she told herself. She'd seen them, the Claytons, and she wanted to know more, get closer. She shook her curls back, giving the wind its head and feeling the relentless Texas sun dancing over her bare arms. Cool air rushed over the same skin counteracting the heat of the sun.

Hitting her signal, she exited right, leaving the highway and following the road to Feathers Inn. With a marked decrease in speed, she turned into the parking lot, speeding to the back, passing an array of cars as brightly colored as the wedding party. She pulled into a space at the rear of the building and cut the engine. The powerful car shut down, leaving a silence that gave her a moment to think about her intentions. Stephanie threw off the negative thoughts and stepped out of the vehicle. She hadn't wanted to be the first to arrive. She wanted to blend in with the crowd, arrive with a group so no one would really notice her and no one would single her out or ask questions about who she was or whether she was a friend of the bride or the groom.

She found the perfect group entering the building. She joined them as they entered the reception hall. Her plan was simple. She'd mingle a while, avoid the reception line, then leave before the bride and groom made rounds to welcome their guests.

Feathers Inn was known for receptions. They catered to weddings, bar mitzvahs, proms, charity balls, anything where the crowd was large and the event elegant. It was the premier place to host an intimate sit-down dinner for three hundred, and the Drs. Clayton-Russell party had the best the inn had to offer. The anteroom was full of people, presents wrapped in white and silver paper, and exotic foods. Stephanie sidled up to a table and tried a dip that was so delicious it should be illegal.

She'd needed something to do with her hands and chose the dip before realizing she was too nervous to eat. She'd never crashed a wedding, never done anything outrageous without Emilie Forester, her friend since college, ring-leading the expedition.

Most of the guests had arrived, but not the bride and groom. She was sure they were staging the obligatory photos. A twinge of jealousy streaked through Stephanie as her mind saw the family assembled with happy smiles as they grinned into the camera. She should be part of the family. She should be standing there next to the rest of the Claytons. Forcing herself to calm down, Stephanie moved about the room, smiling at people, listening to snippets of conversation, but not engaging in any herself. There was no blood between them, she reminded herself. They'd lived with the Claytons while she had not. They weren't family—not really.

Stephanie made her way back to that dip more than once. The third time she reached for a plate and crackers. Someone spoke to her and she filled her plate.

"This is great dip," a man said.

She nodded and whispered, "I've had more than my share."

He laughed, a deep, carefree sound. "Are you with the bride or the groom?" He was dressed in a black suit with a white dress shirt that had crosswise tucks in it. The buttons were pearlized, ringed in black circles.

Tremors ran through her. She'd been caught. Heat flushed up her body from her toes to her ears. She thought she would choke on the piece of cracker in her mouth, but managed to swallow it in time. Then she realized he hadn't been one of the wedding party. She'd scrutinized their faces and his, although good-looking, had not been among them.

"I'm not with either of them," he said, saving her from lying and apparently proud of his conquest.

"You crashed a wedding?" Her eyebrows went up as if she weren't doing the same thing.

"Yeah, I do it all the time."

Stephanie smiled. "You're with the inn, aren't you?"

"Caught." He clapped his hand over his chest mocking a wound. "And so fast. Most people don't get around to that for at least an hour or so, if they figure it out at all."

"I'm a quick study."

"Are you enjoying yourself?"

"So far. This dip is to die for."

"Now, I'd hate for that to happen." He gave her an appreciative wink. "It would be a real waste."

Someone called to him and he excused himself. "I'll tell the chef you approve." Stephanie smiled as she watched him walk away. At another time she'd have pursued him. As it was she hadn't even asked his name. Time was short and she wouldn't be deterred from her mission.

The wedding party arrived. Stephanie's heart stepped up a beat as the reception line formed. The beautiful people came in, smiles all around as if nothing could mar the day. At the end of the line one woman sat in a wheelchair. Stephanie stared at her. Was this Devon Clayton? Was that her mother? Stephanie stared at her, secretly willing her to give some sort of sign that she knew her child was in the room. But her attention was focused on smiling and shaking hands or accepting congratulatory kisses from the guests.

Stephanie scanned the other members of the party. Another woman, in the right age bracket to be her mother, stood at the other end of the line. She looked tired as if the wedding was an ordeal. Her face was marred with lines. She wore a hat and veil to concealed it, but it drew attention to her face more than it deterred it.

Stephanie wasn't close enough to give one of them favor over the other. But she had to know.

She waited, her throat dry and her heart sounding so loud in her head that she could feel the blood pulsing in her temples. Forcing herself to relax, she took a deep breath and released the tension in her neck and shoulders. This would help her headache in the long run. The guests kept coming, more and more of them. The bride should be tired of smiling, but she didn't look it. She was as fresh and dewy-eyed as if she'd just greeted the day.

Stephanie watched from the fringes. Eventually the line wound down. As the last couple shook did not work in an office, had never worked in one, but she was the expert. Stephanie had come across a lot of "experts" in her years as an interior designer and she had learned to treat them with kid gloves. But Mrs. Shulman, a short stout woman with thick ankles, had a smile on her face. Her cheeks were flushed and as red as a Christmas bulb. She wore a brown suit that was very stylish, but not for a woman her age which was somewhere in the fifties.

"It's just wonderful," she said, twisting around and looking at the room. "I couldn't be more pleased."

A sense of relief went through Stephanie and her knees almost buckled. While she was confident in what she did, it always made her feel good to know she'd found the cord in another human being, that when the drawings and models became painted walls and three-dimensional furniture, the clients would like what they saw, even if they couldn't verbalize it when they told her what they thought they wanted. Mrs. Shulman had been very specific in her desires. It helped that her bank account was virtually unlimited. And it had paid off.

"Thank you so much. I was worried it wasn't up to your standards," Stephanie replied, feeding her the ego-booster she required of all those she lorded over.

"Standards. Honey, this far exceeds everything I had in mind when I explained it." She loved to call people Honey. It usually saved her the trouble of remembering their names. "I'll be sure to call Mr. Shulman and tell him what a wonderful, no, marvelous job you've done here." She turned around and surveyed the place again. The windows were tall without any obstruction. Plants were strategically placed in the open area and around groupings of furniture. The lighting was intelligent. It was bright, but would adjust itself to the changing sunlight. On rainy days the lights would compensate.

They were standing in the reception area of the executive offices. The color scheme was a soft blue with rich mahogany paneling that contrasted the brightness of the room. Stephanie had gone for intimate settings, as if business deals would be discussed and decided in the bright Texas sun of the anteroom.

Mrs. Shulman was still surveying the room. She walked back and forth, touching each piece of furniture, each plant, checking the windows. It was the white-glove test, even though she wore no gloves. Stephanie wondered if she were looking for something that was out of place. Then she mentally shook herself for believing Mrs. Shulman had ulterior motives.

"You deserve an added bonus for this." Her words made Stephanie feel even more guilty for her previous thoughts. She walked forward and took both of Stephanie's hands in hers. With a genuine smile she said, "It isn't often I get what I want, but this . . ." She dropped Stephanie's hands to spread hers, her mouth open in hesitation as if she couldn't find the words to express herself. "I will certainly send clients your way."

"Thank you, Mrs. Shulman." Stephanie's business could use more work. She'd been on her own for eighteen months and was only scraping along. This job would put a dent in the red ink on her income statement, but there was much more needed before she felt comfortable. She had dreams of running the premier design firm in Dallas, but she was still in the baby pool. Clients like the Shulmans could help her achieve that goal.

"Rusty will be so pleased." Olivia Shulman's shrill voice, as she referred to her husband, brought Stephanie back to the present. Everyone called Rutherford Shulman, Rusty. He gave the illusion that he was just one of the boys, but underneath that down-home exterior was a ruthless businessman. "He's having dinner at Jake's Friday night with Owen Clayton. Now there's a man who's going places . . ."

Stephanie stopped listening to her. Owen Clayton's name hit her like an exposed secret. Adrenaline rushed into her blood, causing an instant headache. It wasn't unusual that Rusty Shulman should know Owen. Rusty was a very powerful man, heading one of the largest banks in Dallas, and from what she'd discovered about Owen Clayton he was on the ladder to the top.

Owen had several important projects going and was obviously in demand. It was rumored that Rutherford Shulman was the financial backing behind a new building in downtown Dallas. Meeting with an architect at Jake's was practically giving him the commission.

Stephanie felt a little pride in how well the Clayton children were doing. Even with the uneasy nature of her own business, they were all doing something that would make their parents proud. Since the wedding and funeral, Stephanie had discovered that Luanne Rogers was a Clayton too. She was a social worker involved in saving children from abused or lost relationships. Luanne lived in Cobblersville as did her brother, Digger and his wife.

By the time Mrs. Shulman finished her inspection, she was gushing and Stephanie was no longer reeling from the picture of Owen Clayton that Mrs. Shulman had unwittingly put in her head.

Rusty was courting Owen for an important job and Olivia Shulman was lapping compliments on Stephanie. Her ego had taken the elevator up with each accolade.

The two woman left the offices with Mrs. Shulman continuing to fill the air with her voice and her praise. She was a person who talked a lot. Stephanie thought silence must be a problem for her. In another life she might have been a good DJ.

Back in her car, Stephanie headed to her office feeling as if she'd won over the president of the United States. There weren't that many days she came away from a meeting with this kind of elation. And she didn't expect today to be the day when she wasn't reamed out over all the things the "expert" disliked. She'd been ready for Mrs. Shulman, had reviewed her methods of dealing with difficult people, recalled her practical experience from other clients, but she hadn't had to use any of it. She was pleased that everything had gone well and that Mrs. Shulman would tell her friends of the agency's work.

Stephanie had formerly worked for Joshua Bellfonte of Joshua Bellfonte Interiors. She'd left him to start her own design firm, Interiors By Hunter. The two remained friends and Joshua was always there to help her along, give her advice and even send a client or two her way.

Caught by a red stoplight during her drive back to the office, Stephanie looked to her right and saw the wrought iron gates with gold finials that defined the entrance to Crescent Hill Cemetery. She stared at the open gates, her elated mood suddenly cloaked by the dropping of a dark curtain. A lump formed in her throat. That cheated and guilty feeling returned to her. She wasn't sure what she had to be guilty about, but somewhere in her head she thought Devon Clayton had known who she was. Yet Stephanie had said nothing to her. It was the way she said "you" that had Stephanie believing, hoping, wanting her to know her daughter had returned.

Even when she visited Devon in the hospital, for the most part, she'd remained asleep. Once she'd awakened and asked Stephanie if she was the new nurse. Before she could answer Devon had fallen back asleep. At the wedding she'd called for Cynthia. Stephanie knew who Cynthia was, but she wasn't sure that Devon had connected her to Cynthia. Was it the ranting of an old woman nearing death seeing things that weren't there? Pulling back from years of quiet trauma, looking for the daughter who left her and never returned? Often it was said that people called out for loved ones who were dead or for someone who'd caused traumatic changes in their lives. From the papers Stephanie had read and the archived footage of the televised pleas she'd seen, the pain evident on her mother's face said Devon Clayton had been clearly shocked about Cynthia's disappearance.

A car horn blared behind her. Stephanie snapped back to the present. The light was green. Quickly she hit her signal and turned the car into the gated entrance. She hadn't been to the grave site since the burial. Needing no directions, she drove to the place and parked. She got out. The day was cooler than she expected. Texas was known for its heat, but today was comfortably cool with a light breeze ruffling the trees.

She stepped gently on the grass, careful not to tread on any graves. Cemeteries were quiet places and people were often reverent in them. She felt that way, wishing she had some flowers to leave, something to let Devon Clayton know that she was thought of and remembered. She'd had a large family, six children, seven if Stephanie counted herself among them. Devon was sure to be remembered.

A small golden plaque marked the spot, but no stone memorial had been set to let the world know she was a beloved wife and mother. Stephanie sat down on the bench near the grave, feeling strangely weak in the knees. She didn't know Devon, had only seen her a few times. Almost immediately after their encounter Devon had succumbed to a heart attack and eventually died.

Stephanie didn't speak out loud. She sat there thinking, wondering what it would have been like to have lived with Devon and her father, Reuben. Were they good parents? What would Stephanie's life be like if she'd grown up with them? Would she still be an interior designer? Had they missed her? Would she have been given the mother's love her aunt never gave her? And what about the Claytons' adopted children? Would they still have become foster parents and taken in troubled children?

It was a philosophical question. One that had no answer. From what Stephanie had been able to find out about Devon and Reuben and the foster siblings they'd reared was they'd made everyone's lives better. Where would those children be today if Stephanie had not been kidnapped? If they'd been sent to other foster homes and grew up without the loving tutelage of Stephanie's biological parents.

She supposed it wasn't unusual for an adoptee to wonder about the life she'd lost. Stephanie remembered the only mother she had known, the woman who'd stolen her and treated her as her own child until she died. She had only warm, wonderful memories of a loving mother and father.

Her mother had married a year after Stephanie was stolen and Stephanie had no reason to think they weren't her biological parents. Both of them died in a car accident, leaving her and her three younger brothers, half brothers she knew now, to be reared by an aunt and uncle in Dallas.

Her aunt, who had no children of her own, never took to her. She doted on the boys, buying them special toys and making sure she attended every school event and extracurricular activity they had. For Stephanie she was always too busy or work conflicted with Stephanie's schedule. Stephanie wondered now if her aunt's attitude had anything to do with her true parentage.

Her uncle, however, loved her. He took her to practices and sat through all her sporting events. When she went on her first date, he was the one in the department store with her as she picked out the perfect dress. And it was him waiting up for her with a glass of sparkling cider so she could tell him everything that had happened. Stephanie didn't know what she would have done if it weren't for him.

It was partly because of him that she found out who her biological parents were. The weekend before her sixteenth birthday she was taking driver's education in school. To apply for her learner's permit she needed her birth certificate. He was busy working on a junker car he was getting ready for her when she got her permit. Grease had worked its way to his elbows and several smears covered his face. He was sweating and having a difficult time getting the carburetor and timing belt to work together. He told her to look in the metal container on the closet shelf in his bedroom.

Stephanie found the case without a problem. On top were official papers with gold-foil seals embossed by the State of Texas declaring her brothers' birth records. Sitting on the floor next to the open chest, she spread them out and continued looking. She saw her aunt and uncle's marriage certificate. This was the original one. Their ceremonial one had been framed and hung on a side wall near the bedroom door. She found her mother's death certificate. Delicately she laid it on the growing pile beside her, running her fingers affectionately over the paper. On the bottom was her birth certificate. Picking it up, she saw another one, then another. There were five copies. Stephanie frowned. Why so many copies? She shuffled through the pile and found her brother Jared's. There was only one copy. Logan had only one. And Winston. She found only one copy.

Then she picked up her parents' marriage certificate. There was only one copy of it, but the date . . . it was wrong. She looked down again. A large envelope fell off the pile next to her. It had been under the certificate. She picked it up. The label read *adoption*.

"What are you doing here?"

Stephanie dropped the envelope as she jumped at her aunt's angry voice. Meriweather, called Meri by everyone she knew except Stephanie, didn't wait for Stephanie to answer. She rushed across the room and snatched the file and all its papers away from her.

"I need . . . I only wanted . . ." She stammered as she always did in her aunt's presence. "My birth certificate."

"For what?"

"Uncle Jack . . . He's taking me to get my permit." She paused and swallowed. "On Monday. It's my birthday and—"

"Get out of here." She cut Stephanie off.

Stephanie got up. She took a step away from her aunt. "Please," she asked, hoping it would soften the woman. "May I have it?" She kept her voice low and used the proper form of the question. Her aunt was an eighth grade English teacher and she was forever correcting someone's grammar. She sorted through the papers and pushed one into Stephanie's hand.

"Thank you," Stephanie whispered and left the room as if it were on fire. She pulled the door closed and leaned against the wall. Her body was shaking and she was drenched in sweat, but she remembered the date on her parents' marriage certificate. If it was right she'd been four years old when they married.

Did that mean *she* was adopted?

She didn't know for sure. No one in the house ever mentioned the word until one night at dinner when Stephanie brought it up. Her uncle had taken her for her driver's test that day and she passed. Her brothers were excited and everyone, except Aunt Meriweather of course, was talking about places she could drive them in her newly re-conditioned Camaro. They wanted to go for ice cream right after dinner.

Her new permit was in her purse, but they had all looked at it and thoughts of owning it brought thoughts of the papers Stephanie had seen the day she got her birth certificate.

Her courage grew and she gathered the strength to broach the subject of her parentage.

"Was I adopted?" she blurted out as if they had all been in her head and knew the thought processes that brought her to the question. The room went completely silent, yet she saw the look that passed between her aunt and uncle and knew something wasn't as it seemed. "I mean, mother's marriage certificate, the date on it, would mean I was four when she got married. Was my father my real father or did he adopt me?"

"Young lady, I don't want to hear another word out of you about adoption or anything else surrounding it," Aunt Meriweather said, her fork clattering on her plate.

Stephanie felt cowed. She looked at her half-eaten food. It was no longer appetizing. Her elation over getting her driver's permit was swatted as flat as a pesky fly.

"Did Mama get pregnant and my father leave her?" she continued despite her aunt's warning.

"What on earth made you ask that?" her uncle inquired.

"You two. You know something you're keeping from me. Why is the date on the marriage license four years after I was born?"

"Your father did not get your mother pregnant and leave her," her uncle said quietly. No one had to ask her brothers to be quiet. They were listening as if they were about to be told the secret of life.

"Who was he?"

"I don't know," her aunt said, rather too fast for Stephanie to believe her. She did know something, but for some reason she wasn't talking.

"Well, if he didn't leave her, am I adopted?"

Her uncle choked on his iced tea. Her aunt jumped up and began pounding him on the back. Stephanie stared at the two of them. She knew her chances of getting an answer were nil, but she wouldn't give up the subject.

"What did those adoption papers mean?"

"I told you I didn't want to hear that word in this house again. And I mean it, young lady. Now go to your room."

Stephanie dropped the subject. She pushed her

chair back and left the table. Never would she ask
about it again and not a word was mentioned in
the house about adoption from that day to this
one. Stephanie vacillated between stories she
made up in her mind. At times she thought it was
her in that envelope marked adoption. Then she
thought her aunt and uncle had adopted and
something happened to the baby. She was sure it
was a baby.

As she got older her curiosity grew. It wouldn't
let her leave it alone. Time and time again when
her aunt and uncle were out of he house she
would go and look for the file, but the container
was gone. She searched everywhere for it, but
could never find it. Until last June. A month before Devon Clayton died.

Logan, Winston, Jared, and Stephanie were always busy, each working in their own careers. It
was hard for them to get together although they
lived in the same city. Then that June, Uncle Jack
took ill and Stephanie went to see him. Logan,
Winston, and Jared greeted her at the door. During this visit Stephanie saw the file container.
Looking exactly as it had all those years ago. It sat
near the back door in the place they put mail or
packages designated for the post office. She didn't
think this was going to be mailed, but wondered
where it had been all these years.

As her brothers were upstairs with their uncle
and her aunt had just taken a tray up for him,
Stephanie pushed the lock on the file container
and it sprung open with a snap. She lifted the top
and quickly looked around for the envelope with
the single word written on it.

Without hesitation she pulled the papers out of
it. She found her name on them. *She'd* been
adopted. Stephanie thought she was ready for the

news. She'd suspected it since she was sixteen years old, but here with the proof in her hands; she could hardly breathe. She sat down on floor. The envelope hit the table as she went down and aged newspaper clippings fluttered about her like the years of her life falling into place.

With a name and a date, it wasn't hard to find Devon and Reuben Clayton. When she'd first heard about the Clayton children, she thought they were her brothers and sisters, but then there had been a story about Devon Clayton adopting them.

Stephanie had gone to the Internet and looked up Owen Clayton. His reputation as an architect preceded him. She knew he had buildings going up all over the city, that he still lived in the house where their mother had lived and that he was younger than she was by two years. She didn't know how to approach him or even if she should. The Claytons lived modestly, so there was no inheritance that was coming to her. She wasn't after money. She wanted a place to belong. But she knew how families could be. She'd had one of her own as a measurement. They wouldn't take kindly to finding another member they had never heard of. They wouldn't even believe she was one of them. And she had so little evidence to support her claim. The one person who could provide irrefutable proof . . . was gone.

She looked at the grave, with its small marker. *Devon Clayton*, it proclaimed. She wondered if Devon Clayton was a soft woman. What were her flaws, her mannerisms, her likes, dislikes? Did Stephanie have any of them? There were so many things she'd wanted to ask. Her plan had been to ease into Devon's life, not abusively thrust herself into her family; but she hadn't had the chance. Circumstances had taken her option away. There was nothing she could do now except make a nuisance of herself with the other Claytons.

Stephanie got up to go. She supposed she would never know much about them. She could find out what buildings Clayton Architects and Associates were building. She could see Rosa on the pages of fashion magazines and she could look for Dean's name as film credits rolled over movie and television screens, but she would never be part of the family—a real Clayton—part of the bloodline that was her birthright.

I won't be back, she thought. Stephanie wasn't one to dwell over things she had no control of. She couldn't turn time back and prevent the things that had happened to her. She couldn't bring Devon and Reuben Clayton back to life. And she couldn't spend her life wondering what she had missed. She could only pick up the pieces and go on.

And that's exactly what she would do.

Stephanie squared her shoulders and turned to leave, but stopped short as she stared directly into the face of Owen Clayton. He wore a light blue short-sleeve shirt and jeans. His shoes were heavy boots that had seen many construction sites. They were coated in red dirt. His eyes were a clear brown and bore straight into hers.

"Who are you?" He took a menacing step toward her. Stephanie instinctively moved back. Fear sliced through her, cold and solid as a glacier.

"Stephanie Hunter," she replied. She knew her name would mean nothing to him, although him being an architect and she an interior designer they did travel in similar if not the same circles.

"Is that supposed to mean something to me?"

"Obviously not." Her back went up.

"Then why are you here?" Owen asked.

Stephanie said nothing. This seemed to make him angrier. "This is a public cemetery. Why are you here?"

"You were at the hospital." He recognized her. "I saw you leaving. And you were here the day we buried my mother. Now I find you sitting at her grave. Why? What do you want?"

"Nothing," she replied. "I don't want anything." Stephanie moved away. She wasn't prepared for confrontation. She needed to think about what she would say. How much of what she knew was she willing to tell him? The Clayton family didn't need to know about her. There was nothing to be gained by telling them.

She walked toward her car. Owen fell into step with her.

"Why are you here?"

"There are other graves in this cemetery. You only assumed I was sitting by your mother's."

He hesitated for a moment. She could see the indecision in his eyes. It was possible she could have been there for a different person. It was also possible that her presence the day Devon Clayton was buried was for a different burial. While Owen decided which was the right story, Stephanie had time to get to her car and start the engine.

"Just a minute," he called.

Owen walked around the hood. She couldn't run him over, so she sat and waited. He moved to her door, put his hands on the car and leaned down to see her through the window. "I apologize," he said. "I thought you were someone I'd seen before."

"In your mother's hospital room?" she paused.

"In the hospital just before she died. I know now

it wasn't you. You do look a lot like the woman I thought I'd seen."

"You don't know her name?"

"There was a lot of excitement surrounding her. She was gone before I had time to talk to her."

"I've got that kind of face." Stephanie slipped her sunglasses on. "People tell me they know someone who looks like me all the time. Why don't we just forget it." She hoped he didn't recognize her. At his brother's wedding and his mother's funeral she'd had her hair braided in an elaborate style. It was piled high on her head and her makeup was designed for evening wear.

The braids were gone and her hair was straight except for the ends, which curved gently under and framed her face. The style was smooth and sleek and as Emilie had told her could grace the side of a box of cream relaxer.

"All right," he agreed. "How about I buy you a cup of coffee to show there are no hard feelings?"

"Thank you, but I'm on my way to an appointment." She had no appointment. She was on her way back to the office, but she didn't want to spend any more time in Owen Clayton's presence. He had a magnetic personality. She knew that from seeing him across the space of the church at his brother's wedding. Up close he was practically irresistible. Coffee only meant he wanted to ask her more questions. He wanted to know if he'd really seen her in the hospital. She *had* been at the funeral and the burial, although she'd hung back behind the crowd. Owen had penetrating eyes. He was an architect, a man used to taking in space and confining it. He must have seen her during the burial.

"How about dinner? I'll make a mean reservation."

His smile was devastating. Stephanie's heart flipped in her chest. She was sitting down and her legs were weak and heavy at the same time. The word charming must have been invented for him.

"I'm afraid not," she told him.

"Why?"

"Mr. Clayton—"

"You know my name?"

"It was on the grave plate," she told him. "The one I wasn't looking at."

He nodded as if in consent. Stephanie wasn't sure he believed her.

"You were saying about dinner?" he prodded.

"I'm not available," she finished.

"Tomorrow?"

"Afraid not." She shook her head.

"Is there someone else?"

Yes, was on the tip of her tongue. But there wasn't anyone else. So far she'd only skated over the truth. She didn't want to compound the fabrication with a direct lie. "If you're asking about my personal life, I'll only say I have other obligations. Now if you'll move your hands I have to get to my appointment."

He stared directly at her for a charged moment. "I'm sorry for your loss," he said, then raised his hands and moved back.

"Thank you." She smiled at him and drove away. Her heart hammered in her chest and her clammy hands gripped the wheel hard enough for her to break the plastic. What was wrong with her? She hadn't been out with a man in a while, but that was no reason for her body to react to him as if she were in the onset of puberty. Owen Clayton wasn't the last man on earth—magnetic personality or no.

Chapter Two

Owen pulled open the door to Jake's, his favorite restaurant, and allowed Gemma to precede him inside. Soft piano music and the quiet air of conversation gave the place an ambiance he could find nowhere else. He loved this place. It was his element, almost as much as when a new building idea took shape in his mind.

Fine wine, exquisite food, an atmosphere of elegance and a beautiful woman on his arm. He asked for nothing more.

"Mr. Clayton, it's good to see you again." The maître 'd greeted him formally. The tuxedo-clad man nodded and smiled at Gemma. "Your table is ready."

Owen moved aside and let Gemma walk in front of him. He wove through the crowded restaurant, nodding at friends and acquaintances, to get to the table that was his usual. The place was more crowded tonight than it normally was on a Friday. Jake's was a simple name. It had been a steak house once with an open-flame grill and the smell of grease hanging heavy in the air. But Jake got married and his wife turned the place into a white tablecloth and single rosebud establishment. She hired a chef trained in France, removed the grease from the air, and got a food critic to taste their fare. From then on the place was overrun with patrons and it was hard to get a reservation without waiting hours, sometimes days. Owen never had a problem. He'd done the redesign and was assured a table whenever he wanted it.

The maître 'd held Gemma's chair and she sat down. Owen was halfway in the process of sitting when he saw *her*. Stephanie Hunter. He had a head for details and never forgot a beautiful woman's name. Not ten feet from him, she sat smiling at the man across from her. Joshua Bellfonte was the man. Owen felt a tightening in his chest, but refused to give it a thought. Her hair was up. She wore more makeup than she'd worn the last time he'd seen her. And she looked like the other woman. The woman he'd seen at his brother's wedding. The woman who'd helped his mother before Brad had come. She carried her dessert spoon to her mouth and slipped the sweet concoction between her lips.

Owen swallowed.

He looked at the man with her. What was she doing with Josh Bellfonte? He ran through women like a drunk ran through cheap wine. More to prove his masculinity than anything else. He was no Casanova, but women did seem to flock to him. It was that cosmopolitan air he faked. Owen was sure it was faked, but it brought in business for his firm and Owen couldn't argue with the man's methods. No one was hurt and he did a fine job.

"Owen." Gemma had called his name twice before he heard her. "Your menu." He glanced upward. The maître 'd was holding the large black and gold folder already open and waiting for him to accept.

Owen cleared his throat and shot him a quick smile, but Owen's attention was centered, not on the woman at his table, but the one across from him. She wore a black dress, with a single white flower that appeared hand-painted into the fabric on her shoulder. The stem and leaves disappeared down her body. It seemed to reflect against her skin, a reddish brown color that was clear and smooth. She had wide, brown, expressive eyes that the candlelight danced in, a straight nose, and full lips. Kissable lips. The kind that talked to his body in a language all its own. He knew from seeing her at the grave site that her body was curved and rounded, not thin and model-like or straight with dancers legs. She had hips, the kind that said *touch me* in slow motion. And Owen could almost feel his hands rising to the occasion.

"I knew there was something different about you when you picked me up tonight," Gemma said, arresting his attention. "Is it her?"

Owen glanced at Gemma and saw her look at Stephanie and back at him. He took a moment to stare at his menu then up at his date. He *had* been ignoring her and he'd been caught, but Owen Clayton had a Ph.D. in the Study of Women and he knew exactly what to say. "No one holds a candle to you, Gemma."

Gemma smiled, sweeping her long eyelashes down and then up. He knew she would. He knew exactly what she would do and say. She was beautiful, an arm ornament, and more than once his date for some affair or other. Their association was mutual. When she needed someone to squire her around Owen played the ornament. But tonight they were both here for the same reason.

"You know we have a meeting with Rusty Shulman tonight and I let nothing get in the way of business."

Gemma wasn't looking for anything more from him than a good time. And that was the way he wanted it. His eyes strayed back to Josh Bellfonte's date. The smile on her face widened. She had a beautiful smile. He hadn't given up on the idea that she had some connection to his mother. Owen couldn't help wondering who she was and why her path kept crossing his. This meeting with Rusty had only been set up a couple of days ago. There was no way she could know about it, otherwise he'd think she was stalking him.

She stood up then. The dress fit her body like skin. A slit ran up her right leg from ankle to mid-thigh meeting the stem of the painted flower. Black nylon stockings covered legs that peeked out as she walked, giving the impression there was nothing else under the dress. Owen clamped his teeth down on his bottom lip to keep from whistling. Architecture took him to many construction sites and even in this century the appreciation of a pretty woman by a group of red-blooded men was loud and vocal. Owen wasn't one to shout catcalls. Devon Clayton had taught him better than that, but Stephanie Hunter had his baser nature erupting to the surface.

The sensuality with which she glided away from the table commanded his full and complete attention. She held her shoulders straight, her body centered. She moved without hurry like a woman who'd found a path she liked and walked it without checking for obstacles. Owen's mouth went dry and he reached for his water glass, but knew no amount of water would quench his thirst. He'd never thought of a woman in those terms. He'd met many men who had specific directions they'd set up for themselves. It was communicated by their presence, but women he summed up as either going nowhere, totally interested in themselves or so into their careers that there was no room for anything or anyone else. Gemma was totally into herself. But Stephanie Hunter was the exception that disproved the rule. He couldn't paint her into a box as easily as that flower had been painted on her dress.

The other woman didn't have to stalk him. In that dress, he'd follow her.

There he was. Stephanie sucked her breath in slowly so Joshua, her former employer and impromptu date, wouldn't notice her attention to Owen. She saw him as soon as he sat down. He was here supposedly for a business meeting with Rusty Shulman. Stephanie hadn't expected him to come with a date, but from what she'd discovered about him, mostly from Josh, he was a local Don Juan.

Stephanie frowned at the thought. She'd met Don Juans and God's-gifts-to-women before and she had no use for them. That wasn't why she wanted to meet Owen Clayton. She also hadn't expected him to be seated directly in front of her, or that Gemma Lawson would be on his arm. The waiter removed the "reserved" sign from their table as he left. It was time for Stephanie to make her move. She'd wanted to meet Owen on neutral ground. She needed to find out about her mother and running into him, even if it was staged on her part, was the best way she could think of to keep him from suspecting her motives. At the cemetery

she'd been too shocked by his sudden appearance
to formulate questions that wouldn't raise his sus-
picions.

"Excuse me, Josh. I need to go to the powder
room."

Josh nodded as she stood up. Jake's was a place
for more than cuisine. Luncheon business deals
were more the norm than the exception. Dinner
wasn't quite as common, but not unheard of. Stephanie knew Josh had seen several people of influence he could talk to before she returned.

She liked Josh a lot. While she'd worked for him
their relationship had developed into something
like family. They were more than friends, but
never lovers. And Josh was like he had described
Owen, a ladies' man. The two had worked well together and Josh had offered her a partnership, but
Stephanie wanted her own business and she was
good at what she did. Josh, instead of being angry
and vindictive, encouraged her. He even helped
her get started and occasionally referred a client
her way. No one big or influential. In fact, he'd
been surprised when he found out she was working for Olivia Shulman. There was no pretense
that Rusty was the final say. Of course Josh had
sent Stephanie his condolences in the form of
twelve long-stem black roses, his own brand of
humor. He never thought she'd actually please the
most arrogant woman in Texas. But she had.

Stephanie repaired makeup that didn't need it
and checked the hem, slit and fit of her gown before finally leaving the room. Returning to her
table, she spied Owen staring at her with undisguised appreciation. Heat flashed through her as
if she'd been caught naked. She pushed it off to
surprise, refusing to consider any other possibility.
Rusty had joined Owen and Gemma. Olivia Shul-

man was absent. Stephanie thanked whatever powers that be for that little bit of assistance.

She concentrated on putting one foot in front of the other, but her high heeled shoes made her feel unbalanced. She forced herself to remain upright and to walk slowly. Owen held his menu, but his eyes were looking at her, undressing her as she approached. Josh wasn't at their table. He was speaking to someone she couldn't see. She felt no guilt at stopping by Rusty's table.

"Hello, Gemma," she said as she approached. "Rusty." Despite the three of them it was an intimate setting, a dark corner, candlelight shimmering. Stephanie squeezed her jaw at the thought. She relaxed her muscles immediately. Owen had a right to date whomever he chose—without her permission, she added.

Gemma Lawson was a beautiful raven-haired woman who came from Dallas society. Looking like a fashion model, her father was a famous doctor and her mother wielded absolute power over the city planning board. Gemma did nothing except socialize and work on various charity boards. Her features were flawless, yet Owen had openly gazed at Stephanie.

"Stephanie, it's been months." Gemma sat up straight with a huge smile on her face. "I've been meaning to call you." She turned to Owen who had stood up. "Owen, this is my friend Stephanie Hunter. Stephanie designed my father's hospital."

Stephanie offered her hand more because it was the proper thing to do than that she wanted him to touch her. Owen took it and after a simple squeeze let it go. Stephanie felt the warmth of his palm accompanied by a low-voltage sting of electricity. She wanted to looked at her hand to see if she had truly felt something physical, but Owen's next question drew her attention to his deep, rich voice.

"You're a designer?"

"Interior," Gemma corrected. "She's an interior designer."

"Oh," he said.

"Join us a moment," Rusty said, moving around to make room for her. She sat and the two men resumed their seats. "What a coincidence," Rusty went on. He had a wide smile that shone as brightly as his bald head. "I was just telling Owen about you." He looked at Owen. Stephanie followed his gaze. "This is the young woman who redid my office."

"Actually, Stephanie and I have already met—almost."

Rusty wrinkled his brow in confusion.

"Almost?" Gemma asked.

"I didn't get her name at the time, but Ms. Hunter is the woman who called for help when my mother collapsed."

He did remember her. Stephanie kept her features calm, but her insides where screaming. "I just happened to be in the right place," she explained. "I don't think I told you I was sorry to hear of her passing."

"Thank you," Owen said. She could hear the discomfort in his voice and see it in the tightening of his face. There was never a way to express condolences. It was awkward for both the person giving them and the one receiving. "You, too, since you had a similar loss."

"I should have realized you and Owen would know each other," Gemma said, lifting the clumsy moment. "Your fields are so closely related. He designs buildings and you decorate them. It's perfect."

Neither Owen nor Stephanie confirmed or de-

nied Gemma's statement. Technically they should
have met before this, but the world was a small
place and Dallas a big one.

"Well, if nothing else, that's a reason to throw
some work her way," Rusty told Owen. Then he
looked at her. "I've been telling him what a great
job you did for me."

"Thank you, Rusty, but you needn't feel any
obligation to me," Stephanie protested. Her resis-
tance sounded like politeness. That wasn't what
Stephanie was doing. Owen Clayton scared her.
Word of mouth recommendations was how interior designed lived and died. She needed them,
yet working with or for Owen Clayton could prove
difficult. Thankfully, her small shop was not at his
level. He'd need one of the big design firms.

"Bull," Rusty stated before Owen could say anything. "This is how business is done. Contacts.
Obligations. Deals."

"I *would* like to talk to you, Ms. Hunter."

"Stephanie," she said.

He gave her a direct look, but remained quiet.

"Stephanie started her design firm last year,
right?" Rusty asked the question, but left no time
for her to answer. "She's building quite a reputation for herself. Hell, Olivia liked her."

Owen looked at her. Stephanie smiled, embarrassed by the praise.

"Give him a card," Gemma told her. "And you
be sure to call her."

Stephanie handed over the requested business
card, but felt no pleasure at doing it. True, her
business was picking up, but she hadn't come to
Jake's tonight for business. She'd wanted to meet
Owen Clayton on neutral ground. She thought if
she got to know him, she'd learn more about her
parents. She wasn't looking for nepotism.

"I'll give you a call on Monday."

"I know Rusty can be very persuasive, but don't feel you need to call me."

"Bull," Rusty scorned. "Let the man call."

"I said I've been meaning to call you," Gemma took up the cause. "Olivia Shulman has been singing your praises everywhere she goes."

"I can attest to that," Rusty said. "You're all she's talked about for days." Stephanie knew Rusty's wife was relentless when she got on a soapbox.

"You can expect business to pick up dramatically. Despite Olivia's hardness, she has a lot of influence. And she's been peddling your praises at every party this week," Gemma said.

"Good. I'll gear up for it." Stephanie had only left Mrs. Shulman four days ago, but apparently she was as good as her word.

"I'd better get back to my table. I wouldn't want Josh to think I forgot I came with him. We were just about to leave." She stood and took a step back. "It was good meeting you," she told Owen and smiled at Rusty and Gemma before returning to her table.

Stephanie felt the power of Owen's stare as she walked away. His eyes bore into her back like afterburners on a jet plane. Josh stood and put her wrap over her shoulders. The two of them left without a backward glance.

She wanted to look back. She wanted to stare into Owen's intense eyes and see if she could find anything of her parents in them. She wanted to shout at him that he'd been where she should have been. That he'd had a wonderful life with her parents, while she'd been lonely and verbally abused.

But she said nothing. She gave her attention to

the man whose arm she held and walked steadily out into the warm night.

Owen strained as he lifted the box. Sucking in a breath through his nose he blew it out of his mouth, the same as he did when he exercised. But this was more work than jogging through the heated air. He carried the third box to the curb and dropped it.

He was finally cleaning out the house. His sister Luanne, his brother Digger and Digger's wife Erin had come by to help. After a few stories over old photos and trophies, they decided to separate or they'd never get anything done. Owen had been through decades of magazines, found recipes his mother never got around to cooking, sale flyers for clothes or shoes she never threw away, marked articles she intended to go back and read again but never found the time. There were clothes of various sizes from infant to teenage that Owen had packed and stored in Digger's truck. Erin ran a day care center and they had a young daughter named Samantha. If Sam couldn't use the clothes, Erin would see that they got to someone who needed them.

Owen continued methodically going section by section in the various rooms. A week ago he decided to remodel the house. The same night he'd seen Stephanie Hunter in the restaurant. He'd taken Gemma home early. She'd told him he wasn't good company, that he had someone else on his mind. Owen denied it, but she was right. He kept thinking of Stephanie. He couldn't understand his attraction for her. Gemma was beautiful, rich, and came from the right background, if he were into that. Which he wasn't.

But Stephanie.

He knew nothing about her. And that was the problem. He wanted to know more. It wasn't the same kind of information he was usually interested in. There was something different about her and frankly it scared him to death. When he thought of her, his heart pounded and he lost his concentration.

He'd ambled around the big empty house until he found himself in his office drawing new layouts of the living space. It took all his attention, consumed him enough that he forgot about Stephanie as the drawings took shape. By three o'clock in the morning he had a good beginning and the initiative to keep going.

Five days later he had completed the design and liked what he saw. The house was both old and new. The outside would remain virtually the same, but the inside would have new rooms and a more open layout. He'd knocked down a wall in his mother's old room and widened it to include an upstairs office. He'd move his things in there and buy all new furniture. The new design would allow him to move into it and not feel he was sleeping in his mother's room. He wondered what the family would think of it. He wouldn't change anything without their approval. Even though they'd given him complete control of their mother's estate and signed over the house to him, Owen still considered this the family home.

Picking up another box he headed for the curb again. He hadn't called Stephanie. He'd been tempted. Several times he'd pulled out the card she'd given him, but never dialed the number.

"Earth to Owen."

He dropped the box and turned.

"What's up with you?" Digger asked. "I've called

you three times and all you did was stare into space. And holding a heavy box at that. Who's on your mind?"

"Sorry; I was thinking about something."

"You mean someone?"

For a moment Owen thought of telling him, unburdening himself of the feelings that Stephanie Hunter evoked in him. He decided against it, unsure of how to put words to what he felt. "No one in particular," he answered the question. "Why don't we go inside and see how Erin and Luanne are making out?"

Digger didn't say anything. He didn't have to. They knew each other well enough to know when something was bothering one of them. And when it was the right time to press for an answer.

Owen turned and headed back for the house. Both he and Digger joined Erin and Luanne on the second floor. Luanne was sorting through papers while Erin packed a box with clothes to be donated. Owen saw the dress his mother had worn to Brad's wedding. He said nothing about it as Erin folded it neatly and placed it in the cardboard box, but he found he had to force down the hard lump in his throat.

"What's going on in here?" Digger asked.

Luanne and Erin looked up from their tasks. Luanne was on the floor, surrounded by piles of papers and photographs.

"I'm organizing a hundred years' worth of paper," Luanne exaggerated. "I don't think mother ever threw out a single scrap."

"I'll help you," Owen said, stooping down and lifting a pile from the floor next to her.

"I've got insurance papers, bank statements, old checkbooks, birth certificates, passports, crayon drawings and who knows what else." As Luanne spoke she pointed to each pile in turn. "And old photographs." She picked one up. "Digger, you're gonna love this one." She extended it toward him. "It's of you in the school play when you were fifteen." Luanne laughed. "You were so bad. And that costume."

Digger snatched the photo and shoved it into his pocket.

"Let me see it," Erin asked with her hand out.

"No way," Digger snapped with a good-natured smile.

"Please." Erin pushed out her lower lip the way their daughter, Samantha, did when she wanted her way.

"Maybe," he said. "If you're good. If you're really, really good, I'll let you see it in ten years or so."

Erin swiped the air with her hand, but missed Digger who spun away from her playful gesture.

Owen easily read the papers and put them in the designated piles Luanne had organized. More insurance papers, more photographs. He smiled at one of himself and Brad right after they'd come to live in this house. Placing it on the stack, he lifted an envelope and suddenly stopped. Around him the banter of friendship and love continued, but the voices of his family receded into white noise and then total silence.

Someone must have noticed he wasn't playing the childish game. He also wasn't listening to the conversation going on in front of him or even looking at it. He was sitting stock still as if he'd suddenly been flash-frozen in place. He held a single piece of paper in each hand.

"Owen?" Luanne called. He heard her voice, but she sounded as if she were talking through water. "Are you all right?" He didn't respond, but continued to stare at the paper as if it were alive. "Owen?" She called again. "What's wrong?"

He looked up. Digger and Erin had stopped joking and all three of them were staring at him.

Slowly he looked at them one by one. From the looks on their faces his must be completely washed of color giving his dark skin tone a grayish tinge. He swallowed, knowing that for the first time since he was a child he thought he was going to cry.

"Owen," Digger said softly, bending his knees and squatting to his level. He reached for the papers in Owen's hands. He let them go as his brother closed his fingers over them. Digger turned them around and read. Then slipping to the floor he sat down with his arms resting on his knees. "We need to call a family meeting," he said, never taking his eyes off the pages.

"Why?" Luanne asked.

"We have another sister."

Chapter Three

Owen never missed a week of going to see his mother. After Brad discovered her last year, the bond between the three of them had been restored. Initially, Owen had had trouble with addressing her, but they had worked out something. Mariette Randall had been moved to a private hospital in Dallas and eventually to the small house she lived in now.

"Mariette," Owen called when he got no answer from the doorbell. He had a key, but had never used it. Everyone deserved privacy and unless he felt there was a medical reason, he waited her for to come and open it.

When she didn't come after a second ringing, Owen walked around to the back. She was bent over a row of yellow flowers.

"Mariette."

She turned to look at him. "Owen." He went to her, helping her up from her knee pad. She had a spade in her gloved hand, a wide-brimmed hat and had been planting flowers. Mariette loved gardening and her efforts showed the beauty of her work in the expanse of color and design that comprised the backyard. "I didn't expect you today." She hugged him as she always did. Owen had the feeling that each time she saw either him or Brad, it was a homecoming all over. So much of their lives had been separated. "Come in, I have some iced tea in the refrigerator."

The house was blessedly cool. "You shouldn't spend so much time outside in the heat," he told her.

"I won't melt. And I find it relaxing." She washed her hands and poured them full glasses of tea. With her hat still on her head, they sat down at her kitchen table. A bowl of fruit acted as a centerpiece. Owen pulled off a section of grapes and popped a couple in his mouth.

Each time he saw his mother, his real mother, Owen felt as if he were a small boy again. That they were back in the cramped apartment and he was eleven years old. Memory had him smelling the odors of food from other apartments when he and Brad had been so hungry. Then she hadn't been beautiful, but compared to the way she looked now, she was Miss America then.

There was a sadness about Mariette. Owen knew she was always happy to see him, but inside her was a sorrow that was deep and hard to break through.

"What's that look for?" she asked.

"What look?"

"The one on your face."

She'd always had the ability to sense when something was happening to one of her boys. Owen wasn't sure if it were a parent thing. His Mom and Dad also had that same ability. Owen remembered the talks he'd had with his Dad when he discovered girls. When something was going wrong. And even when he was on a winning streak.

"The good news is that Brad will be here tomorrow."

"Wonderful." Her face lit up. "It'll be good to see him again. Will Mallory be with him?"

Owen nodded.

"Family meeting?"

He nodded again. "Do you want me to come and get you or will you join us through the screen?" Mariette had the electronic equipment. Dean had set it up in her house. She rarely attended the meetings, saying they were really for the children and that they would do what was best.

"What's it about?" she asked.

"We were cleaning out Mom's things yesterday." She waited intently. "We found some papers. Apparently, before they took in foster kids, they had a daughter. She was kidnapped at three years old."

Mariette gasped. "Kidnapped."

Owen related what he knew of the story.

"I vaguely remember it now," Mariette said when he finished. "Cynthia," she said as if she were trying to remember the child. "Her mother was crying on the television screen." She looked up at Owen. "You weren't even born then.

"I know. The dates on the newspaper clippings we found would make her thirty-seven now." Owen was only thirty-five.

She drank her tea. "You better come and get me for this one."

Even though the Claytons were spread across the lower forty-eight like random clouds banked over a vast landscape, they all got to Owen's as fast as the speed of light when he called with news that another Clayton had been discovered. The family had at Dean's urging, since he was frequently in faraway places, begun using a video conferencing process from wherever they were located to attend family meetings. But the discovery of an unknown sister warranted an in-person meeting and they'd descended on Texas like supersonic war birds.

Newspaper clippings, worn photographs, birth certificates that had been folded and refolded many times littered the table in the Clayton family dining room. The story of Devon and Reuben Clayton's kidnapped child, Cynthia, was laid out in print. Owen felt the tension in the air. Unspoken and unanswered questions echoed around the room as surely as if they'd been shouted in a cavern. He'd gone over them in his head since the discovery of the documents. How could his parents have kept this from them? Why did they never speak of a daughter? They'd been so loving to their adopted children, guiding, nurturing, explaining, and sometimes even yanking them back to the straight and narrow, but in all that time they didn't breathe a word about a tragedy that ripped their child from them.

Owen had relayed the story by phone to his brothers and sisters who hadn't been present when the contents spilled out of the manilla envelope, but he'd gone over it again as they assembled across the table from each other. When he finished, the silence stretched like a taut band. A family secret that must have caused intense pain for their parents.

He watched his family get up and spread out as if they suddenly needed more air or more space to take in what had been said.

"This sounds like something I would write into a script," Dean said. It was his way of trying to relieve the tension in the scene. Owen had seen him do it many times in the past. "Why didn't they tell us?"

The room had taken on the oppressiveness of a wake. Brad stared through the window. The sun shone brightly outside, but he had the look of someone who didn't see it. His mind was probably lost in a past memory. Luanne and her husband Mark sat at the table. Between them was a pitcher of iced tea and several partially filled glasses. The glasses were as abandoned as the people in the room.

Dean paced about as if the room were a large cage and he could only go so far before having to turn around and retrace his steps.

Digger, never far from his wife, Erin, leaned against the wall near the kitchen doorway. Erin sat on a stool next to him. Her hand lay lightly on his arm. Owen felt the two gave each other strength, that together they completed each other and he remembered how they had come to almost lose each other and lose the love that was as obvious between them as the black newspaper print on the aged paper.

"We don't know," Erin finally answered Dean's question. "There could be many reasons; pain, fear, even hope, but we'll never know the real reason they never told any of you."

"We lived with them since we were children. All my life," Rosa said, her voice appearing strained and hurt. "In all that time, they never ever mentioned a child. I don't understand."

"I know," Owen said. "We thought they couldn't have children. That was why they took in foster kids."

"All the while." Luanne picked up a color photo of a smiling two year old. She and Mark had no children, but Luanne was the director of children's welfare in Cobblersville. "All the while, they had a daughter. A real daughter, a biological child. They must have been distraught."

Luanne had witnessed families in crisis before.

She'd seen children taken from abusive relationships and known the hardships it scarred them with. Equally, she'd been there for reunions of parents and children who only needed time to pull their lives together. Owen didn't have to wonder if she'd been party to a situation like the one they faced now.

"What do we do about it?" Owen asked. He'd done nothing but think about the missing Clayton daughter for the last two days. He needed to do something now, act on the knowledge they had gained.

"We have to find her," Dean answered positively. Owen had expected Brad to make that statement. Brad was his biological brother and the two of them had been abandoned as children. Brad had spent twenty years searching for their biological mother. Yet Dean spoke quickly and without hesitation.

"How?" Brad asked, turning from the window. "This is not a two-hour movie. The police tried to find her what, more than thirty years ago. And we're supposed to do it now?"

"You found Mariette after twenty years." Dean's voice was soft as if he didn't want to fling Brad's successful search for his birth mother in his face." They all turned to look at Mariette, who sat quietly watching them.

"Do you know how long it took me to do that? Do you think we have time for another one?"

"You had less to go on then than we do now." Dean picked up one of the pieces of paper from the table. "We have her name, a photo—"

"She won't look like that now," Rosa said.

"No, but there is aging software." Dean looked at Luanne. "We can get a good guess of what she looks like now." As a child welfare director, Luanne dealt with lost and found children, but also knew the people in the Missing Persons Department. She was surely able to get them to do a favor for her and age the photograph.

Luanne nodded.

"Dean, don't get your expectations up," Brad warned. "It could take years if we can find her at all."

"Well, we have to do something. We can't just sit here. Mom and Dad wouldn't want us to do that." Dean's voice was rising.

"Then why didn't they ever tell us about her?" Brad countered.

"Let's not fight." Owen held up his hands. He knew how his strong-willed brothers could get and he needed to head off any argument they might get into. "We can hire a private investigator. See what he can come up with. At least we'll make an effort to bring her back into the family."

He looked around the room. In turn each family member nodded.

"We can ask the guy who found Mariette," Owen said. He had called Devon Clayton mom. When his birth mother was found last year he was torn with feelings of disloyalty for the woman who'd been his mother in every way except biology. Mariette suggested he call her by her name, which she said she needed to get used to hearing after so many years.

"Would you like me to call him?" Brad asked.

"I'll see to it," Owen told him. Brad had used a detective to find their missing parent. Owen thought it best if he took on the job this time.

Brad moved from the window and picked up two glasses to take them to sink.

"Cynthia," Owen said quietly. "Find, Cynthia."

"What?" Brad stopped close to him.

"Those were Mother's last words. At your wedding, she clutched my hand and made me promise to find Cynthia."

"It's was perfectly natural," Brad told him. "She had a daughter named Cynthia and when she was dying she called for her. It happens all the time."

Owen nodded, but in the back of his mind he was thinking of someone else. The other woman. Stephanie Hunter. She'd been with his mother in the bathroom. Did she know anything? Why had she been at the wedding? And the funeral?

Why had she sat at his mother's grave site?

"You did what?" Emilie Forester asked. She and Stephanie had just stepped into the huge rotunda of The Women's Museum when Stephanie delivered the bombshell. Emilie stared at her as if she'd suddenly grown another head.

"A drive-by." Stephanie flippantly threw the words at her friend and headed for the bar across from the floating stairway that led up to the second and third levels. She glanced at the *Words on the Wall*, but had read them so many times she could recite the twelve quotes if asked. The sand colored structure which housed many artifacts detailing the accomplishments of American women had had many tenants in the past, including a livestock auction, the Texas Centennial Exposition administration building, the Goodyear Tire and Rubber Company, a warehouse and several others until 1996 when Cathy Bonner spearheaded its renovation and made it the repository of female art in America.

The interior had a warm blond colored floor with high walls in subtle colors that defined space and brought it to a smaller scale. The ceiling rose at least a hundred feet in some places. Stephanie looked up as she always did when she was here. The moving activity of people and space drew her attention into all the spaces at one time.

Ordering two glasses of white wine, she gave one to Emilie and the two moved toward the stairs.

"Hunter, you're a stalker," Emilie whispered, drawing her attention back to sea level. Emilie was a service brat and always called Stephanie by her last name. She'd lived in more countries than Stephanie could find on the map and spoke several languages. She said they helped in her work as an emergency room nurse.

"I am not," Stephanie denied. "I only drove by the house to see what it looked like."

"Did anyone see you?"

"I don't think so."

"You don't think? So there was more to it than a simple drive-by?"

"They appeared to be cleaning out the house."

"They?"

"There were several cars in the driveway. I saw Owen place a box at the curb among many others that were already there waiting for trash pick-up. I was so tempted to stop and see what he was throwing out."

Emilie put her hand on Stephanie's arm. Her fingers squeezed tight and her fingernails dug into Stephanie's flesh. "Tell me you didn't?"

Stephanie stopped on the landing. "I didn't. I didn't," she said quickly. Emilie released her hold with a sigh. Then taking a sip of wine Stephanie glanced over the balustrade at the Electronic Quilt, a thirty-foot-high matrix of television screens with illuminated photos, quotes, colors, and video cubes comprising both still and moving images from the museum's exhibits.

"It *was* tempting though," Stephanie teased.

Emilie's face was a study in seriousness. "What were you thinking? You crashed the wedding, spent time in the hospital room, went to the funeral. How long do you think it will be before one of those men or women get so curious they have to find out who you are and why you're stalking them?"

"I am not stalking and this *was* your idea," Stephanie countered.

Emilie's free hand went to her hip. And she assumed the position; head cocked to one side, chin lowered, eyes wide and accusing. "Don't go throwing this one on me. I only asked you a few questions. Who knew I was building Frankenstein's monster?"

Stephanie made a face at Emilie Forester. Then she smiled. Emilie was her best friend. As college roommates, Stephanie had confided in Emilie about the adoption papers she'd found as a sixteen-year-old. Emilie was adopted, too, but unlike Stephanie she had always known it. Her adoptive parents had not kept it a secret. She's mentioned it one night during a floor meeting in the dorm. Stephanie's head had come up when she said, "I'm adopted." She'd been intrigued by Emilie and gravitated to her due to the commonality of their existence. She wanted to talk to her, ask questions, finally be able to say out loud some of the questions that plagued her.

Emilie was more curious about the discovered papers than Stephanie. They tried to find out who her birth parents were, but to no avail. When Stephanie discovered the truth of her kidnapping and adoption, Emilie was the first person she called. And it was Emilie who suggested she find out about the Claytons. In fact, Emilie looked up Owen Clayton and discovered he was an architect

living in Dallas, only a few miles from where
Stephanie lived.

At that point Stephanie had become as curious
as Pandora and opened the box that had her, in
Emilie's words, "stalking" the Clayton family.

"I'll bet it's one of those guys. One of those *fine*
guys, I might add. That's what you're after." The
hand on the hip was gone and both now surrounded the wineglass as Emilie leaned her elbows
on the wall ledge and looked over at the expansive
floor below. The permanent exhibits at the museum included a history of the accomplishments
of women. Tonight the gallery was hosting a private showing of the works of Isabel Robinson, a
combination of paintings and photographs mainly
of families. Hundreds of people milled about study-
ing the walls, examining the oversize photos or the
massively colored canvases, drinking, talking, and
laughing. The rich and influential rubbed shoulders with the up-and-coming. It was amazing how
large Dallas could be, yet how small the town really
was.

"Don't be silly," Stephanie said, turning her attention to the floor. "They're practically my brothers."

Emilie turned her head slowly and looked at
Stephanie. She shook it from side to side. "Not a
single one of them?" Each word was said individu-
ally, giving them all weight and emphasis. "Their
bloodlines don't mix with any of yours, not even if
I dig past the six degrees of separation."

"Well, I'm not romantically interested in them."

"Yeah, right." Emilie rolled her eyes. "I've seen
them and they could raise the blood pressure in a
statue."

Stephanie couldn't help but smile. "So it's you
who's interested in one of the brothers."

"Let's see, Brad just got married." Emilie ignored Stephanie's comment. "James is also married. Dean is a little young for you. That leaves—" Emilie's eyes opened wide and her brows went up.

"Stop."

"Oh, yes, Owen; that long, tall drink of water for a thirsty woman. And you, my friend, are dying to imbibe."

"That is not my intention," Stephanie said, but she didn't sound convincing.

"It's all right, girlfriend. If I were you, I'd guzzle the man down without the slightest bit of hesitation."

Stephanie held her friend's gaze as long as she could before they both burst into laughter.

Stephanie turned and had her foot on the step, prepared to continue her ascent to the visiting exhibit on the top floor when Emilie's hand on her arm stopped her. She turned back and looked at Emilie, who was staring at the floor below. Following the line of her gaze, Stephanie froze. Her stomach fell as if she were in a plane that suddenly dropped altitude. The wineglass in her hand shook and she quickly steadied it. Below them a band played in the far corner of the room. Throngs of people dressed in black evening clothes danced on the natural flooring. And the broad shoulders of Owen Clayton and his brother James were clearly visible among the museum's inhabitants.

"What's he doing here?" she whispered as if speaking in a normal tone would allow him to hear her.

"It's an opening," Emilie stated. "Art, architecture, influential people; sounds to me like a place Owen Clayton would want to be."

Stephanie didn't like the smile on her friend's face. It was like some competition between them and Emilie had gotten the better of her. Stephanie didn't know why her body reacted to seeing Owen the way it had. Her mouth went dry, her stomach dropped and she trembled. The two had been talking about him and suddenly he was there. It was just the act of surprise that made her react, she told herself. And it wasn't sexual. Her symptoms were those of fear. She knew she was making her presence too coincidental. After a moment, she had herself more in control, but sipped her wine to wet her throat.

"Did you know about this?" Stephanie indicated the dark head of the man on the floor. He'd just thrown his head back in laughter at something a woman said to him. Stephanie looked closer. He was talking to Olivia Schulman. And at that moment she looked up and straight into Stephanie's eyes. Her face lit up and she gestured for Stephanie to join them. Owen turned and looked up then and Stephanie felt pinned in place.

"I've been summoned," she whispered again, unable to throw her voice more than a few inches. Owen wore a black tuxedo with a white shirt and instead of a tie, a thin black band circled the short mandarin collar of his shirt. The man was devastatingly attractive. From her vantage point he should appear shorter, but the long lines of the jacket and pants and the fact that he towered above Olivia set him apart from those around him.

"Time to pamper Olivia," Emilie chided. "I'm going to go on up." She glanced up the stairs. "See you later."

"Coward," Stephanie growled before starting down the stairs. By the time she reached Olivia and Owen, James was dancing with his wife. The two gazed into each other's eyes and Stephanie could tell the room might as well have been empty as far as they were concerned. They only had eyes for each other.

"Stephanie, this is Owen Clayton." Olivia introduced. "He's a very gifted architect."

"We've already met," Owen said, nodding to Mrs. Shulman. Stephanie remembered that deep voice.

"That's right. Rusty told me she stopped by during his dinner meeting with you. Well you've seen the work Stephanie did for Rusty. She's very good. Owen, you should use her agency for some of your projects. She has an eye for detail and will give you more than you expect."

Stephanie smiled, embarrassed at the compliment and at the way Owen's eyes were encapsulating her.

Someone caught Olivia's attention and she waved at a woman across the room. "I have to go talk to Gerry Mathis over there. The woman is the worst bore I've ever met." She glanced away and smiled brightly at a bejeweled woman in a stunning green gown. "You two talk." She looked from Owen to Stephanie. "I have more people for you to meet tonight, so don't get lost." Her comment was for both of them.

She left with a smile as if she were meeting her best friend. They watched her cross the room for a moment. Then Owen turned to Stephanie. "Did she say bore?" he asked. Stephanie held her teeth together, then she smiled. A moment later they both burst into laughter.

"Maybe we'd better dance?" Owen offered. He held his hand out. She put hers in it and they both hesitated a moment. Her eyes went from their hands to his eyes. A titillating thrill ran through her, forcing her to still it before she could take a step. Then they moved to the floor near the band.

The song was slow, with a moody saxophone blowing low sexy notes. She turned into his arms as if in a dream. Somewhere in her mind a voice told her to be careful, not to move this fast, fall this quickly, but it was drowned out by the rushing blood in her veins and the fact that only the emotional synapses were firing in her brain.

"It seems everywhere I go these days I run into you," Owen said next to her ear.

"Really," Stephanie hesitated, but her heartbeat increased a pace or two. "I hadn't noticed that."

Owen leaned back and looked down at her. "If I didn't know better I'd swear you were chasing me." Stephanie gave him a stern look, but his words were close to what Emilie had said and very near the truth of her actions.

He turned her around the floor a couple of times before broaching a different subject. "Olivia believes I should use your firm. The offices you did for Rusty are impressive. I have a number of projects in the works. Maybe I can send some work your way."

This was the way things were done. Josh had schooled her well in this respect. And Rusty had reinforced the technique. You network wherever you go, he'd said. It used to be called washing each other's backs, but Stephanie couldn't let that image take hold in her mind. It was already out of control from being folded in Owen's arms and smelling the warm scent of his aftershave. When the music stopped, even though she'd already given him a business card, she fished in her evening bag and pulled out one with her name and logo on it and handed it to him. He glanced at it before slipping it in his pocket.

If you want something, ask for it. She could almost hear Josh's voice whispering in her ear. "My firm is fairly new, Mr. Clayton," she told him. "And I would appreciate any business you'd send my way."

"Owen," he said, with a disarming smile. It wasn't a dazzling smile, but she felt it shine into her.

"O-wen," she said.

People jostled them as the music started again. Placing his hand on the small of her back he led her away from the floor and toward an empty table on the edge of the crowd. A waiter passed them before they reached it and Owen snagged two glasses.

"I hope you like champagne."

She was thirsty after the dance and her nearness to him. She wanted to drink deeply, but forced herself to sip the bubbly wine.

"You said your firm was new; how long have you been in business?"

"Two years." It was stretching the truth, but he didn't need to know that. Two years sounded better than eighteen months.

"Did you come to Dallas then?"

"No, I was born here."

It occurred to Stephanie that she was beginning an alternate history of her life at this moment. She had believed she was born in St. Louis. It was where her mother had lived. And no one had ever corrected her or said any different. It was when she had seen the newspaper account of her kidnapping that she discovered her real birth place.

And her real family.

"I used to work for Josh at Joshua Bellfonte Interiors. A couple of years ago I decided to go out on my own."

He was nodding. "I know Josh. I'm surprised we're only meeting now." He smiled again and Stephanie had to steady her heart. "But, since we've run into each other several times, maybe we're trying to make up for it."

"Maybe. To paraphrase a very old-black-and-white movie, the world is a small place, but Dallas is a big one."

"You like old movies?"

"Love 'em."

"What's your favorite?"

"*Casablanca.*"

"Ah, a romantic."

"Insatiable."

"What about you?"

"I'm more the guy-action movie type; *The 39 Steps, Twelve O'clock High, African Queen.*"

"That was in color, made in 1951, directed by John Huston."

"So you like guy-action type movies too?"

She nodded. "I appreciate those, too. You know, I once worked for a client who wore hats like Kathryn Hepburn in that movie. The one where she wanted her niece to have a lobotomy."

"*Suddenly Last Summer?* You're kidding?"

Stephanie shook her head. "The woman I worked for had crippling arthritis and wanted an elevator in her home decorated to reflect the days of her youth."

Stephanie was wondering how she could bring the conversation back to him and his family. She knew she was bordering on the obsessive, but she really wanted to know more about them.

"Are you the only one with this love of old movies? Or does it run in the family?"

"I suppose I get it from my mother."

Stephanie held her breath. He'd gone exactly where she wanted him to go. She had to force herself to let her breath out slowly, normally, as if the word *mother* didn't hit her like a cannonball to the gut.

"She used to teach me lessons from the movies;

honesty, doing for others, the power of laughter."
His mouth tilted at the past memories that must
have flashed through his mind. Stephanie wished
she had some of them to share with him.

"She must have been a wonderful woman."

"The best," he said. "When videocassettes came
out she'd buy them and at her beck and call she
could immediately begin teaching."

"What about you?"

"My college roommate. Many Saturday nights
would find us with a bottle of cheap wine, watching old movies while everyone else was out on a
date."

"By choice?"

"Occasionally."

"I can't believe any man would let you stay home
alone." His voice was full of charm. Stephanie steeled
her emotions not to give way to him, but electricity
prickled under her skin.

"Let's just say there was a shortage of men."

He took her hand and pulled it close to him.
"We'll have to remedy that."

"Did your mom teach you that, too?" She pulled
her hand free.

He didn't get the chance to answer. At that moment they were joined by his brother James and
his wife.

"For a moment there I thought you'd ditched
us," James said. He came and stood next to Owen,
his wife holding onto his arm.

"May we sit down?"

They took the free seats and Owen introduced
her to Digger and Erin. "Stephanie is a decorator.
She did the new Shulman offices."

Erin nodded as if she knew about it. Stephanie
silently thanked Olivia Shulman for her penchant
for telling everyone how pleased or displeased she

was with someone's service. Thank heaven in Stephanie's case, the story was positive.

"Erin is on the board here along with our sister Rosa." He pointed across the rooms, indicating the museum's board. Stephanie looked at a tall woman with long dark hair flowing down her back. Clearly the most beautiful woman in the room, men were gathered around Rosa as if she were a life-giving nectar.

As if she could feel their stares, she turned and glanced toward the table. Her smile widened before she returned her attention to the male harem.

"If it weren't for these two dragging me here, I'd be spending the evening with a building project."

"Sure, Owen," Digger said. "It's Saturday night?"

Date night, Stephanie thought. But for Owen any night could be date night.

"Deadline," he said. "You know I'm serious about my work. And I'd just had an idea when you called."

"You could have brought Dean."

"He had plans. And you already had a ticket."

And a date. Stephanie could hear it in the unsaid silence. She knew Owen's reputation and she'd seen him with Gemma Lawson. If the rumors she'd heard were true, Owen Clayton always had a beauty on his arm.

Digger turned his gaze to Stephanie. "You look familiar." His brow wrinkled. She could tell he was trying to focus on where he'd seen her before. Panic attacked her. She took measures to control her sudden lack of breath. For the first time tonight she wished she'd worn something other than the strapless gown, something body-covering, something that wouldn't so visibly show the rise and fall of her breasts.

"Ah, two charmers in the family." Stephanie

played for time. "Does it extend to all the Claytons?" She glanced at Owen.

"Absolutely," Erin answered, smiling broadly at her husband.

"But once you get to know them, they settle down to being merely irresistible." They all looked up. Rosa stood there with only one of the beautiful men. She was wearing red and it suited her. Everything was red, the gown that molded to her body like satin ink, her panty hose peeking through the thigh-length slit, her shoes; even the ribbon threading through the stand-up braid crossing her crown like a tiara atop a cascade of hair was red.

They pulled up chairs and joined the growing members of the Clayton clan. Only a couple more and the entire family would be present. And she would be among them. Stephanie wondered what they would say if she told them she was one of them? Almost one of them. That the woman who'd raised them was her real mother.

Hearing Owen speak her name, she realized he was introducing her to Rosa and her date, Bob Morrison.

"Where did you two meet?" Rosa asked, her stare direct as if she were interviewing Stephanie for a job she had no intention of giving her.

"Over by the bar," Stephanie answered, nodding in that direction. She wanted to distinguish herself as independent of Owen's usual women. While Stephanie wasn't model-beautiful like her adversarial would-be sister, and she wasn't willowy like Gemma Lawson, she didn't really have designs on Owen. She wanted to know more about the Claytons and she wanted to know about her family—the one she'd lost. These were the only people who could provide that information.

"Believe it not," Owen interjected, "we were discussing future business arrangements."

The table was quiet for a moment as pregnant as if an unexpected silence had muted the room. Then the three Claytons erupted in laughter. Digger leaned back in his chair, threatening to fall off the seat. Erin gripped her wineglass as a high note rose on the air. Rosa's expressive hands waved in the air like a conductor directing a symphony.

Heat washed over Stephanie. The rust-colored pigment, usually an underlying tone in her brown skin, glared to the surface, turning her exposed skin into blushing sheets.

"I apologize, Stephanie," Erin said. "Owen has a reputation of being a ladies' man."

"Yeah," Digger continued. "Him sitting here with a beautiful woman"—he indicated her—"... and discussing work is hard to imagine." Mirth punctuated his ability to get his words out.

"You're giving Stephanie the wrong impression," Owen defended.

Digger answered him with a skeptical look. Stephanie glanced over her shoulder. She wondered if Emilie was still on the top floor. Then she saw her. On the landing where the two of them had stood half an hour ago. Emilie watched Stephanie sitting with the family she longed to have. The word "stalking" jumped into her mind as if the multicolored electric quilt was flashing it for the entire association to witness.

"I'm sorry," Owen said. "We must be monopolizing you. I never thought to ask if you were alone."

There was a question in his last statement. For a moment Stephanie wished she could say she was with someone. She suddenly needed protection.

"I'm here with a friend." Deliberately she neglected to say if her friend was male or female. She left the decision in his mind and knew he'd choose the opposite sex. Had she seen a scowl on his brow, a slight narrowing of the eyes?

"Maybe we should dance, Erin," Digger suggested. Erin rose and took her husband's hand. The two left the table. Rosa remained, continuing her scrutiny of Stephanie. Digger might not have noticed his sister's hostility or protection, whichever she deemed it, but Stephanie could feel the vibrations. The young beauty was not finished with her. Bob Morrison had said little past his introduction. She wondered if Rosa always overshadowed the men in her presence.

"Do you decorate commercial properties or private residences?" The question had the earmarks of innocence, but Stephanie was no fool. Rosa was probing, leading, searching for something. Insecurity gripped her. Had Rosa seen her at the funeral? Did she know her real identity? Were those the reasons she was sitting at this table instead of being the nucleus inside a cell of adoring men?

"Both," Stephanie answered. "My office is on West Holiday." It was a high-end section of town, established businesses, prestigious. Not in the old money—the oil money—area of the city, but the first place the rich came for services. They could move from caterer to florist to decorator to maid services to anything they needed in one place. Getting space on West Holiday was either inherited or commissioned at birth. Stephanie had Josh's recommendation behind her and the community allowed her entrance if not acceptance. Until she received the Shulman commission, she was on trial. And now that Olivia was in her corner, the inner circle was embracing her. "My clientele is small, not exclusive. I'm working on expanding it.

Before starting the firm I worked with Joshua Bellfonte Interiors. And I'm good at what I do."

Rosa's flawless skin darkened until it rivaled her red costume. "Does that include picking up men?"

"Rosa!"

"Rosa!"

Both Bob Morrison and Owen spoke at once. Owen's voice held a warning. Bob's surprise. Her eyes shredded them.

"It's all right, guys." Stephanie stood. The men followed suit. "Apparently, Rosa is in protection mode."

"Protecting whom?" Owen asked.

Stephanie gave him a piercing look. Turning her attention to Rosa, she smiled, hoping it was both engaging and disarming. "You needn't etch a single worry line because of me. Your brother and I share only dependent professions." Slipping her rhinestone-crusted evening bag under her arm, she addressed the men. "I really must go. I have yet to see the exhibition. Good night."

Her eyes lighted on Rosa who remained seated. The soft face that looked at the world from countless magazine covers with smiles that were sexy, beguiling, or innocent, was absent tonight. Her expression was stony. Stephanie pushed back and walked away. She didn't turn back and look for she was sure Rosa's stare would turn her into a pillar of salt.

Chapter Four

Owen had his hand on the phone. It had gone there constantly this morning, but only twice because it rang. Digger had called to say he and Erin were safely back in Cobblersville. Owen had snatched up the receiver as if he expected it to be someone else. The person on his mind. The one who'd occupied it since he'd first seen her.

Stephanie Hunter.

She didn't have his home number or the separate office line he maintained, so the idea of her phoning him was both erroneous and moot.

When he woke up this morning his first thoughts were of her and Rosa's obvious hostility to her presence. Owen couldn't remember his sister acting that way before. And Stephanie had left them without a backward glance. For some reason that had irritated him. He was used to women vying for his attention, verbally sparring for his heart. But Stephanie Hunter had simply laid the facts out, and like one of the movie characters they'd discussed, made a simple and graceful exit.

Owen mentally shook himself. What was wrong

with him? He wasn't the type to settle on one woman. They were as interchangeable as roofing tiles. There were only a few who could be trusted and he was related to them. Taking a seat at his drafting table for the third time that morning, he went back to working on the idea that had come to him the night before.

He'd been immersed in it when Digger called to remind him of his obligation to attend the museum opening. Then Tiffany Yarborough had cancelled their date due to illness. This morning he had time, but his concentration seemed to be broken. The idea kept getting sidetracked and his mind kept drifting. He was thinking of Stephanie Hunter.

She might have been discussing decorating last night, but he wasn't thinking of that. His mind was on the way her body felt wrapped around his, the warm kiss of her breath near his ear as they danced. The music had held them together in a timeless dance. He could still feel it. If he raised his arms, he could hold them at the precise level where she fit into his body. Emotion slammed into Owen, the impact that of a raging tornado. The essence of scent that surrounded her crowded his senses. It wasn't strong, overpowering or even memorable. It was haunting, like something in a fog he couldn't quite bring into focus. Yet it held his interest, forced him to concentrate to gather it close when he knew it had the consistency of moonlight. But it was sexy in the extreme.

Owen was used to seducing women, used to pursuing them to his own end, playing with them as if they were toys; but Stephanie Hunter was a different caliber woman. And Rosa had felt it, for her reaction was that not of a sister, but a jealous lover.

Owen's hand still played over the phone. Simon

Thalberg had called. He had a report for Owen and would meet him at three. Usually he would have insisted on Thalberg giving him the details now or meeting him right away, but instead he thought of Stephanie. A three o'clock meeting gave him time to call her. Invite her to lunch. Use the excuse of apologizing for Rosa's actions.

It was easy to dial the number on the card she'd given him. It lay on the desk in front of the phone. Owen's problem was he'd never wanted to call a woman this bad. He'd grab his phone book and quickly call someone, securing an escort for the evening with as much effort as it took to walk across the room. Yet this morning he'd reached for the phone ten times and not dialed it once.

Disconcerted by his own reaction to a simple action, Owen jumped when the phone rang under his hand. Swallowing, he let it ring twice. Then clearing his throat, he answered it, expecting one of his siblings who called often. If he wasn't in his office downtown, they knew he was working at home and had a separate number from the private house phone. This had been done for convenience when his mother was alive. He could work at home and make or receive calls without competing with her busy schedule of friends and charities.

"Owen Clayton," he said.

"Hello, this is Stephanie Hunter."

Owen nearly dropped the phone. He sat up straight and shifted the receiver from one ear to the other. "I'm glad you called." He paused. "I wanted to apologize for my sister's rude comments."

"Thank you. I fully understand her motives. I hope you don't mind me using this number. I tried your office and they said you were out."

"How did you get it?" He was curious. The number wasn't a secret, but he didn't include it on his business cards, mainly because when he was home, he wanted privacy. Yet he'd given it to clients in the past.

"Josh dropped in and he heard me talking to your secretary. He gave me the number."

Owen made a mental note to thank Joshua Bellfonte when next they met.

"I'm calling to follow up from our conversation on Saturday night."

She was all business. None of the soft woman he'd held in his arms and danced with Saturday night was apparent in the voice on the other end of the phone line. Yet Owen's reaction to her was the same. He sat back in the chair and remembered them swaying to the music, their bodies in unison as they communicated on a universal level. A sheen of sweat suddenly covered him.

"Which conversation?"

"The one about working. You're the architect on the new Dallas Herald building. I know it's late, but if you haven't already contracted with a design firm for the interior I'd like to bid on it."

"Bids are still open," he replied. "But they'll be closing in a couple of days."

"Is that Wednesday?"

"Yes." He nodded as if she could see him.

"Good, then I'm not too late. Is it possible for me to get the specs for dimension and requirements?"

"I'm working at home today. I have a set of them here—"

"Would you mind if I came by and picked them up," she interrupted.

She was aggressive, Owen thought. The quality didn't repel him. In fact, he liked that about her.

Go for what you wanted was his moto. It had gotten him where he was. The fact that she was a woman made it more exciting in his mind. He loved to see women get ahead. His sister Rosa's behavior Saturday night was in character with someone who fought for what she wanted. Fiercely loyal to the family, Rosa would stand up like a hellcat in a storm to keep any threat away from it. At twenty-six years old, that pugnacity had made her one of the top models in the world.

"Can you make it at noon? We can have a few minutes to go over some of the changes that haven't been updated on the copy."

She agreed and rang off.

Owen had been about to tell her he could fax it or E-mail it to her office, but when she offered to come by, he couldn't resist the opportunity to see her again.

The Clayton home had been updated to bring it into the siding-on-three-sides-brick-on-the-front decor that was prevalent in the newly constructed areas of the city. The landscaping was designed to be natural, but to Stephanie's trained eye it had been elegantly manicured to show off that effect.

Owen opened the door as soon as she rang the bell. He'd said he was working at home. She expected him to be dressed in jeans, sweats, khakis, something comfortable, but he was wearing a suit and tie. At the museum he'd been under lights designed to show off the paintings or exhibits. Today it was broad daylight, high noon, and the gray suit contrasted with a light blue shirt, and a matching striped tie fit him as precisely as the lines on an architectural drawing.

"Am I on time?" she asked.

"Yes, come inside."

She stepped over the threshold. Stephanie held her breath. It had been a bold move coming here, working her way into the house. She hadn't planned it from the beginning. When he said he was working from home she jumped at the chance to see the house. It was like walking into a dream. Nervous tension made her hands cold and her body hot. Her internal temperature outmatched the central air-conditioning by at least ten degrees.

"I hope you haven't eaten," he said as he led her into the living room. "Since it's lunchtime, I was about to have something to eat. I hope you'll join me."

"I'd love to." Stephanie hid her surprise. She expected him to meet her at the door, already have marked the changes and hand her the papers. He'd said he was serious about his work and she knew how deeply she could concentrate when developing an idea. But she was glad she would be spending time with him.

From the staircase in front of her, a wide polished wood construction with intricately carved spindles and a newel post that had the sculpture of a woman, came an energetic young man in his twenties loaded down with luggage. She recognized him as Dean Clayton, the youngest of the brothers.

"Hi," he said, sticking his hand out. A computer bag on his shoulder slipped off-balance, falling down his arm and yanking his hand too low for Stephanie to grasp it. "Sorry." He set the case on the floor and offered his hand again.

"My brother Dean," Owen introduced. "He's a film producer and is constantly on his way to the airport."

Dean glanced at his brother. "Lucky for you." He looked directly at Stephanie when he said it.

"I'm sorry I won't be here," he told her. "This film is a great opportunity. Maybe we'll meet again?"

"Maybe," Stephanie said, although there was a sort of don't-count-on-it note to Dean's comment. Stephanie knew it had to be Owen's non-entanglement with women that he referred to. Emilie had given her the low-down on Owen and the women he dated. Although how an emergency room nurse knew what she knew was beyond Stephanie. And she was *not* a date.

Dean lifted his computer case and rubbed the head of the newel post. As the door closed on Dean's departure, Owen's hand on her lower back sent a shiver down her spine. He led her through the house. The rooms she passed through or saw, as he walked her from the foyer down the hall, were huge. In the living room the air had a light scent of lemon wax. It held a long piano covered with photographs. Stephanie only had a moment to glance at them, but she could see the family in various stages of growth. The dining room was formal and on the opposite side of the kitchen. She could only see what the rectangular doorway allowed. The table in the kitchen had been set for two. She looked questioningly at Owen.

"I assumed you'd be hungry."

"You were right." She'd rushed to get through what she was doing at the office to get here on time. There was really too much work. She was going to have to hire someone soon, even though she could barely afford to pay a decent wage.

Owen pulled out her chair. Stephanie hooked her purse over the back and sat down.

"It smells delicious. What are we having?"

"Enchiladas, refried beans, rice, tacos. I hope you like Mexican food."

Her mouth watered at the delicious aroma of

the food. Owen opened the refrigerator and pulled out a pitcher of iced tea. He filled her glass. Stephanie took a sip while Owen opened the lids on several pots and began making a plate. She got up and went to him.

"Let me help." He smiled at her, but didn't move. The stare went on so long Stephanie began to feel awkward. "What?" she asked.

"For a moment you reminded me of my mother." A streak of fear passed through her. "I didn't mean that," he rushed on. "Not the way it sounded. She taught us to help out. You kind of did it without thinking."

Stephanie was required to help out at home. Often she cooked for her brothers since her aunt and uncle worked. She wondered what type of women Owen went out with if they didn't join in and help with small details. Gemma Lawson had probably never been in a kitchen. Maybe that was his type. Stephanie picked up a taco shell and began to fill it with shredded meat, lettuce, tomatoes, and cheese, topping it with extra taco sauce.

"You miss her, don't you?" She kept the conversation geared toward his mother.

"She and my father were the greatest influences in my life."

They finished making the plates and took seats at a table designed for many more people than the two of them.

"My real mother, my biological mother, was missing for over twenty years. My brother, Brad, found her last year. The Claytons took us in and loved us as if we were their own."

"Why did your mother leave you?" Stephanie knew she shouldn't have asked. "I'm sorry. That's a very personal question. You don't have to answer it."

"She was attacked," he continued as if she hadn't

spoken. Stephanie gasped. "Beaten badly, unable to speak or remember anything. My brother and I were put in foster care. We continually ran away until we were placed here." His voice was flat, but the kind of flatness that was reached for, like an actor speaking words to hold back the emotion of hurt.

"I'm so sorry," she said when he finished.

"She's better now. Living alone. Taking care of herself. I see her often."

"What's she like?"

He hesitated a moment, thinking. A look came over his face that Stephanie couldn't read. The closest she could get was confusion. "When she didn't come home that day . . . I was eleven . . . I was so scared. She loved us. I know she did, but then we couldn't find her. And people came and took us away. She'd never find us if we weren't where she left us.

"When we came here, Mom, we called her Mrs. Clayton then, she told me that nothing about my mother's leaving was my fault. It took years for me to believe that. When we eventually found her, it was like suddenly I could see that for the years we had suffered, she had done so, too. Not knowing what happened to us was killing her. I think she's unhappy. When I'm with her I feel like she regrets missing so much of our lives, but there is no way to get that time back."

"What about grandchildren?"

"What?" She caught him by surprise.

Stephanie kept her face expressionless and sipped the iced tea. "I mean your brother, Brad, right? He's married. I'm sure grandchildren will help her forget some of the pain of missing your childhood. She'd have the chance to do it with them."

"I'll tell Brad that when I talk to him next." His smile was mischievous. He cracked a taco as he ate it. Stephanie could see some of the boyishness in his expression and was glad the heavy mood was broken. She also wondered why he'd told her so easily about something that must be painful to remember and to live with.

"Maybe we'd better let them make that decision on their own," she conceded.

They finished eating and she watched Owen clean the dishes and stack them in the dishwasher.

"It was an unexpected meal," she told him as they headed back toward the foyer. "But I enjoyed it."

"I always enjoy food better with a pretty lady."

The charm was back. He'd given her a glimpse into the real Owen Clayton when he talked about his birth mother, but now the ladies' man was back in habitation.

"Maybe I'd better take those papers. I'm short on time if I want to get my bid in by Wednesday."

They had reached the living room. "Wait here, I'll get them."

She heard his footsteps going down the hall. His office must be one of the rooms she'd passed. Stephanie took time to look around. The room was done in beige and soft greens. One wall of the room was a bold hunter green. Centered on it was a faux fireplace with a gas element under realistic-looking fake wooden logs. The piano sat in one corner angled into the room. Stephanie was drawn to it as surely as if it were a giant magnet. She let her eyes skim over the photos, going from one to another, not alighting on any of them for longer than a few seconds. The frames were varied and many styles, from glass to playful shadowboxes. They were in no particular order. From the left she found high school graduation photos next to toddlers and young boys playing on swings. She recognized Owen smiling from atop a ladder leaning against a building under construction. He must have been in his teens.

There was Rosa, as beautiful a little girl as she was a grown woman. She had an innocence about her that she retained. It came across in her photographs, visible from the covers of magazines. Stephanie didn't try to place the other family members. But then she came across a small framed picture of Devon and Reuben—her parents. Her hand was reaching for the frame before the action registered in her brain.

Finally, she thought, after ten years of knowing they existed, she'd found them. Stephanie expected something to happen to her. She thought her heart would well up with emotion. That tears would pour down her face, silent tears or giant sobs, long and wet. Something that would stun her, make her feel closer to the people who had given her life. But what she felt was numbness, the lack of all feeling, like the world had suddenly stopped spinning around the sun, as if there was no wind, only a frightening stillness that bubbled around her body and paralyzed her in place.

"Sorry it took a while," Owen said as he entered the room. Stephanie had her back to him. "I made a few updates and printed a fresh copy."

The bubble over her burst and Stephanie gently set the picture back on the piano. Gathering her strength she turned to face Owen, most of her senses back in place when she walked the few steps to where he stood.

She accepted the manilla envelope containing the papers and slipped it under her arm. "I'd better let you get back to your work. Thank you for the meal and for allowing me to enter a bid." Her hand touched the envelope. She turned back and looked around the room, her eyes taking a last look at the photo of her parents. She knew it was time. She'd said good-bye, taken the papers she'd come to get, but now that she was inside the house she wanted more than a brief glance of what her life could have been; she wanted to wrap herself in the alternate history.

Stephanie Hunter was the same woman who'd occupied his vision and his mind since Saturday night, but the woman in front of him was different. She was dressed for business in a yellow suit that set off the underlying red in her skin tone. Yet that sensual quality of her movements was ever present. She was probably unaware of it, but it was like a scent that drew in the male animal.

And she wore it well.

Owen searched his mind for something to say. Something to keep her here for a few more minutes.

"This is a lovely house," she said. Owen had seen her admiring the architecture of the rooms. He watched as she looked around at the room. He saw the dark wood columns that separated the living room from the formal dining area. "Your family must have had a wonderful time growing up here." Her glance was through the distant dining room windows on the large backyard.

"You've only met Digger and Rosa. And Dean on his way out," he added.

She spread her free arm and turned a full circle around. "There are photographs all over the room." Owen looked back at the scene Stephanie must be seeing. On the piano, the end tables next to the sofa, even the entertainment center had a shelf of photos. They were the remnants of his childhood. Owen hadn't thought about them, rarely even seen them. They were part of the room, part of his world, so much so that they'd become invisible. But to a stranger they must seem numerous.

"We had a lot of fun here," he finally answered. For a moment Owen was a child again. He remembered racing down the upstairs hall and rushing down the steps to get to the Christmas tree. If it hadn't been for his mother and father he never would have had that memory, and he didn't even want to think of what would have become of him and Brad if they hadn't ended up in this house. And what would have become of the others? They'd truly been lucky.

"How many are you?" Stephanie interrupted his thoughts. He snapped back.

"Six," he said. "Four boys, two girls. What about you? Do you have any brothers or sisters?"

"No sisters, three brothers."

"Older? Younger?"

"All younger."

"I'm sure you had your share of fun times as kids."

"We did. For a while we lived in St. Louis. All my brothers were born there. Then we came back here."

Owen felt more than heard the change in her voice. He wondered what the real reason was for her returning.

Stephanie took a step toward the door. He knew it was time for her to go, but suddenly he didn't want her to leave. He'd prepared lunch to keep her here and now she was about to walk out.

"This is really a lovely house," she said again. He heard a sadness in her words. You're very lucky." Then she started moving toward the front foyer.

"Would you like the grand tour?"

She stopped. "If you have time and don't mind. I never get tired of looking at houses, especially the older models. They have a lot more character than the new cookie-cutter development houses."

"I'm thinking of remodeling it. Maybe you can give me some decorating advice."

"For which room or rooms?"

"Why don't I show you my plans. I believe the whole place needs an update." He led her down the hall to a cramped little room that had been their father's den. When this house was built they still had dens. In newer homes the small den was now a huge family room. They already had a family room. It was one of the add-ons he, Brad, and his father had put onto the house.

Owen rolled out the plans for the lower level on his drafting table. Stephanie walked around and stood in front of him. He could smell the shampoo she used, a pleasant floral scent that went straight to his head and tightened his body in all the right places.

"You're removing this room to make the kitchen and dining room larger." She glanced at him with her hands on the page. He nodded. Saying anything was beyond his capabilities. "Do you entertain a lot?"

"Not a lot. The family is expanding. In the last two years we've had two weddings and one adoption."

"So you're not remodeling in hopes of selling?"

"What gave you that idea?"

"It's my profession. I often consult with homeowners who want to get the most for their homes. A little polishing here and there, new wallpaper, spruce up the rooms, makes it more attractive to buyers."

"This is the Clayton house. It'll always be in our family."

Owen hadn't meant to be so emphatic. Stephanie probably didn't know what it meant to be homeless, to finally find roots. This house represented more than a home. It was a haven, a place where the wounds of six people had been uncovered, cleaned and healed. The four walls didn't make it a home, but the lives that had been nurtured and guided, thrived deep down into the base-wood, the Sheetrock, and the earth on which the structure stood.

Stephanie had given her attention back to the plans, rolling the blueprint over and holding it with her left hand while she studied the rendering of the upstairs. She looked at the pages with a comfort level that told him she'd done this countless times before. And her reading the first floor, understanding exactly what the plans said had him respecting her ability.

"This is the master suite." He reached around her, careful not to let his arm make contact with hers. He pointed to the drawing, but the heat of her body was intense in its closeness. "I've removed a wall from here to expand the room and my office will be in this area."

"There are six bedrooms now."

"More, if you count the attic. There will be the same number when I finish."

She looked up and smiled. She was close, too close. Owen froze. The need to kiss her was stronger than it had ever been, yet something inside him wouldn't let him do it. He moved his eyes from her face, from the softness of her mouth, to her hair. It was loose about her shoulders, shining in the light from the windows. He wanted to touch it, possess it. He didn't understand this sense of propriety. Usually he would move in for the kill. He'd seduce her, maneuvering her into this position, and when she looked up with those eyes that dripped chocolate, he'd have hesitated for the sake of acting, letting her believe this was a spontaneous act, borne of the attraction between them, when it was planned and calculated as precisely as the plans on the desk.

But he didn't. Instead he said, "Maybe we'd better continue the tour."

She stepped away from him, but not before he noticed that their proximity had an effect on her, too. She bowed her head as she moved, but Owen felt the slight tremble in her movements. Her hand brushed his and it was as cold as ice. He smiled, hoping she was as out of character as he was.

The staircase was wider at the bottom and curved slightly as they ascended. The house didn't call for a huge formal staircase and Owen had always thought this one was perfect for the space.

"This post was carved by Digger." He pointed out the newel post.

"Who's the model?"

"He wouldn't tell us, but we suspect it was his biological mother. Digger was thirteen when he came here. He'd been living on the streets and stealing to survive. Seeing that he had an aptitude for working with wood, Dad suggested he try wood sculpting. This is his only effort. It isn't very good, but he was proud of it and the two of them installed it here. We named her Clare and we all rub it for good luck each time we leave the house."

"I saw Dean do that before he left. I suppose it

accounts for the smoothness in certain areas," Stephanie stated.

"And that there were boys in the house." The head was very smooth, but the breasts and buttocks had also received their fair share of pubescent hands.

As they ascended the stairs, Owen pointed up. "We used to run along this hall and slide down the banister. We had to be careful to get off before reaching the post." He laughed. "Often the momentum would have us crashing into the wall or falling on the floor. My parents were forced to carpet the hall to keep us from killing ourselves."

"It looks like fun." Stephanie noticed the hall carpeting was gone and stained wood flooring gleamed in the midday sun.

Owen opened the farthest door. "This was Brad's room."

"He's the doctor?"

"You were at his wedding."

"I was in the same hall," she corrected, then added, "I couldn't help looking in. Weddings are always so beautiful. They're irresistible."

Brad's trophies were still in the case Digger had built for them when he was in high school. The bed had a dark blue spread on it and the desk was as neat as it had been when Brad had studied there.

He took her to Luanne's, and Rosa's rooms then Digger's who shared with Dean, before showing her his.

"This is my room."

While Stephanie had stepped into the other rooms and looked around, this time she only looked inside from the doorway, staying on the hall side of the threshold.

"It has a lot of character."

He moved on to his mother's room. She did go into this one. She walked to the center, looking at everything. Owen thought she looked as if she were in a sanctuary. She touched one of the posts of the bed, ran her hand along the bedcover and stared at the pillows as if his mother was still lying there.

Owen walked up behind her. He was careful to stay out of the range of her scent, as if invisible hands would pull him to her.

"I'm sorry," she said softly. He felt as if she were speaking to his mother and not to him. And he heard tears in her voice.

"It's all right. You saved her life." It was her time, he thought of saying, but didn't.

"But she died," Stephanie said.

Her voice was far away. He knew she thought of the person she had lost. This room must have brought the feelings back. They did for him. A wave of emotion went through him. He saw it in her, too, and couldn't stop himself. He turned her into his arms. She was soft and he liked the feel of her. Her arms encircled his waist and she rested her head on his shoulder. Owen ran his hand over her back and up into her hair. He held her against him, losing the battle he was waging to keep his mind clear and his body from reacting to hers. He pressed his lips against her hair and was rewarded when she relaxed in his arms, her hands tightening around him.

Owen kissed her temple and her cheek. He inhaled deeply, taking in all the perfumey smells that mingled together, but finding the one that was hers alone. It drove him on and he slid his mouth over hers. Owen had kissed his share of women. In fact, he'd gone well over his allotment, but at no time had sensations ripped through him like they did when Stephanie's arms ran up his back and her body pressed into his.

Owen should have pushed her back. He was used to ending relationships that got too serious. He hadn't known Stephanie long enough for their relationship to develop, let alone get serious, but it was reversed this time. He was getting serious, too serious and too fast.

Yet he didn't stop. He folded her closer to him, deepening the kiss, sweeping his tongue inside her mouth and forgetting everything on earth except how good she felt pressed into him. Heat surrounded them. Owen was sure they would spontaneously combust within seconds. But suddenly he was thrust away from Stephanie.

She jumped back, her hands going to her heart. Her eyes were wide with fear and something that looked like shame.

"I'm sorry," she said in a breathy voice. "I shouldn't have done that." She quickly looked about the room and then headed for the door.

"Stephanie?" he called, following her a second later. "What's wrong?"

She sped along the corridor and started down the stairs. She hurried as if someone were chasing her.

"Stephanie, stop."

She kept going. At the bottom of the stairs she headed for the door. Owen took her arm, but she wrenched it free and continued.

"I'm sorry, Stephanie." He didn't know what he was apologizing for. She was as much into the kiss as he was, but something happened that he didn't understand. "Would you stop and talk to me?"

She stopped on the porch, but didn't immediately turn to face him. Owen breathed hard. He stopped when Stephanie did, afraid to get close to her. If he got too close she'd run to her SUV.

After a moment she faced him. Taking a deep breath she spoke. "Owen, I apologize. It's not you. There are things about me you don't understand and I can't explain." She took a step backward. "Just let me go and forget anything ever happened."

She left him then. Owen watched her retreating steps as she moved to the SUV at the curb. He didn't try to stop her. He stood on the porch watching the empty space as Stephanie's vehicle disappeared around the corner.

What had happened? He'd never scared a woman with his kiss before. At least not after he'd gotten out of high school. Yet she'd run. He should be glad. She was exactly the kind of woman he steered clear of—the marrying kind. She had home and hearth written on her as clear as indelible ink. Yet when he saw her at the door, his heart lurched so violently he thought it would jump out of his chest.

Holding her in his arms, kissing her, had been heaven. But that was the last of it. He wasn't in the market for marriage. He'd decided that years ago and while Digger and Brad had fallen, it wasn't for him. Stephanie Hunter was past tense, over before anything began. That was the best way.

Owen turned and walked back into the house. He closed the door and stood still, shocked that he could still smell her perfume.

At three o'clock in the afternoon Jake's was between lunch and dinner and not very crowded. Still, as Owen entered the place there were at least three people who asked him to join them.

"I'd love to, but I have a business meeting," he told them, shaking hands, kissing cheeks, and making his way to the table where Simon Thalberg waited. He sat with his back straight, and his hands folded as if he were in grade school and afraid of breaking a rule. Menus lay in front of Simon and an empty seat where Owen would sit. Owen had the feeling the older man had already decided on his meal and only waited for him to make a decision.

Simon Thalberg had begun his career as a New York City cop. Before being wounded in the line of duty, he'd made detective. In his fifties, he had gray at his temples and thinning hair across his crown.

Owen slid into the seat in front of him. "Thank you for meeting with me," Owen said. The two men shook hands and a waitress appeared. Owen expected Simon to order coffee and nothing more, but while his selection was basic food, it was nevertheless substantial; a thick hamburger with all the toppings, French fries and the expected coffee. Owen asked for the same.

"Have you found anything?" Owen was anxious, more than he thought he would be. He had a full family, four brothers and two sisters. He didn't need another sister and maybe she was secure in her family, too, even if she had been kidnapped. Maybe the people who took her, wanted a child so badly they stole her and treated her well. But he knew better. Most of these stories ended in tragedy, children being abused or neglected. Maybe she was dead and that was why no ransom had ever been offered for her return. Owen had prepared himself for this kind of knowledge.

He hadn't, however, looked ahead to what would happen next. Luanne was a child psychologist and he'd call on her if needed. He'd called her last night to let her know he was meeting with Thalberg today and that if his fears proved true, they might need her services and more.

Owen thought of them finding his birth mother last year. Her story of abuse had been horrific. It had touched him more than he thought possible. What had Thalberg to tell him today?

"I find that I often remove the appetite of my clients if I give them the details before the meal. If you don't mind, we should eat first."

The waitress brought their coffee and Owen watched as Simon added milk and a sugar substitute to his cup. Owen drank his black.

"How did you get into being a private investigator?" Brad had told Owen that Thalberg was wounded in the line, but never the details.

Thalberg raised his left hand. There were four fingers, but no thumb. "I lost it in a gun battle with some drug lords in New York." His voice was stoic, without emotion, as if he'd separated this story and the actual happening into two parts. He could relate it without reliving it.

"Were you in vice?"

He shook his head. "Homicide was my area, but the two often overlapped. It was a routine call, dead body in an abandoned building. The place was alive with cops and cars when I got there. Then suddenly the dam broke, DEA agents came out of the woodwork. NYPD uniforms were all over the place and gunfire lit up the darkness. When it was over, I woke up in a hospital, digits"—he held his hands up, palms out—"numbering nine."

His story didn't help Owen's apprehension. It was another story that didn't have a happy ending. But, Owen thought there was a silver lining, and he grasped for it. For the common man, retirement and disability would be the order of the day, but Simon used it as the opening of another door. He went into private investigation and found he had a knack for it. Maybe whatever he had to tell Owen wouldn't be so bad.

"I'm surprised you'd still want anything to do with law enforcement."

"I don't look at it like that. I don't accept divorce cases, peeking into windows to let a spouse know her partner is cheating. Mainly I'm in missing persons. Sometimes my work ends happily. Sometimes it only provides closure, but either way it allows people to begin a healing process. It's as close to being a psychiatrist as I can get."

It was a different aspect of his service. Their food arrived and they dug in like college students whose every meal was their last. To think that Owen had only finished lunch two hours ago didn't keep him from eating heartily.

Cleaning his hands on the warm finger towel the waitress left on a small silver tray, a trademark of Jake's, Owen pushed his plate away and pulled his refilled cup of coffee closer. Thalberg must have taken it as a signal for he started his report.

"She wasn't hard to find."

"You've found her already?"

He nodded.

"Is she alive."

"She's alive."

"You said at our first meeting it might take years to find even a word about her."

"Luck was on our side. Cynthia Clayton was also looking for her birth parents. She went to the national registry of adopted children and put her request in. She left a name and address."

"What is it?" Owen involuntarily held his breath.

"Stephanie Hunter."

* * *

"Damn." Owen slammed his hand onto the railing of the cage that would take him to the top floor of the building under construction. Things were spinning out of control and he couldn't stop them. He'd pulled his tie free and opened the collar of his shirt after getting the file folder Simon Thalberg had left with him and reading through it. It was incredible. Stephanie Hunter was Cynthia Clayton. She was someone he knew.

He left Jake's, but couldn't go home. She had been there. Her presence was still in the air. Images of holding her in his arms and kissing her in the upstairs room were burned in his mind. And her fragrance hung in the air. He needed to think, needed to decide what to do next, how and what to tell the family.

He'd come here, to the construction site. To a place where things were defined by girders, nails, screws, beams. Where a straight line held no interpretation, where windows only came in a finite number of styles. Where angles met and mitered. And there was no room for secrets. No place for hidden meanings and unexplained actions.

Owen had no idea how he got to the site. From the look of his dusty shoes and the rumpled way his clothes clung to his sweaty body, he'd walked. His suit no longer reflected the image that most of his friends would recognize as his. Stephanie was on his mind, but she also occupied his subconscious. While he couldn't remember getting to the site, this was the *Dallas Herald* building, the same building that Stephanie had come to get the interior specifications.

"Damn," Owen cursed again, accompanying the words with the slamming of his hand. "Damn,

Damn." He couldn't believe it. There had to be a mistake. Or a huge coincidence, and he didn't believe in coincidences.

Owen didn't know how long he remained there. The cage had stopped on the top floor, incomplete, without walls or a roof. No work was being done at that level. Stepping out of the construction elevator, he removed his jacket and tie. He rolled up his sleeves and sat cross-legged on the floor.

The stars were over his head and the lights of downtown Dallas surrounded him when he became aware of his state. He'd sat oblivious of the heat or the sun. Finally, it was time to go home. He couldn't avoid the world forever. Stiff legged, he got up and tested his cramped limbs. Stepping into the cage, he pushed the solid red button and the small craft began its descent to sea level.

He had to walk several blocks to find a taxi, which took him home. His car was still in the parking lot at Jake's. He'd get it tomorrow. Tonight he'd call Brad.

But when he got home there was another surprise waiting for him.

Stephanie put down the last page of the specification notes. She'd read them three times and had the beginnings of an idea of what she thought would be a good fit for Owen's building design. But Owen's face kept intruding. And her hasty exit. She couldn't imagine what had been going through her mind. Owen was a client. How on earth had she ended up in his arms? And why did she feel as if she belonged there?

She knew his reputation. He dated a lot, but no one for any length of time. After she discovered her true parentage and casually asked about the Claytons, time and time again Owen was the most known, both for his designs and for his reputation with women. Obviously, each of the women had thought she was the one to rope him in, but found trapping him elusive.

Stephanie wasn't in the market. Despite her being folded into his arms like wrapping herself in a velvet winter cloak that had a steel latticework concealed inside it. The feel was soft to her skin, but the bands holding her were secure, sure, and strong.

Stephanie shook herself, trying to force her mind back on the idea for the interior of the Dallas Herald's new building. She'd visited the old building several times, placing ads, and once being interviewed and photographed for a story about her and the opening of her business. Her professional eye couldn't help taking in the lines and angles of the rooms she saw, the placement of desks and cubicles. She thought the setup workable, but could be improved. Reporters needed privacy for creating their stories on tight deadlines, but they also needed to be able to reach out to each other, not to feel that they were writing in a cell or room with no windows. Cubicles, in her opinion, were demeaning.

She remembered Owen's office. It was set with his back to the windows. During daylight he'd cast a huge shadow over his drawing table. He should turn it to the side so the light flowed across the surface. Pulling a piece of graph paper toward her, she counted off the rough dimensions of the room and placed the door and windows. Then she set about arranging the existing furniture to provide the best light and functionality for working and accessing work tools. There were a few photos of previous projects leaning against the wall, which she would hang. Then she added a multilevel lighted case that rotated like the file system in doctors' offices where space was at a premium. This would hold three-dimensional mock-ups of the structures and surrounding areas he'd completed. His own private museum. Of course, she would have to have it custom made, but it would clear space while being accessible at the push of a button. She knew people who did the impossible and this wasn't close to being that complicated.

What she found impossible was the way her mind kept returning to Owen's mouth on hers. But it was more than that. It was the secret. She didn't like them. Since discovering her family held a secret and they'd kept it all her life, she hated things that were hidden, not brought out and made available to the people they affected.

She hadn't told Owen she knew she was related to Devon and Reuben Clayton. Telling him would do nothing except cause hard feelings that were unnecessary. Stephanie only wanted to know about her parents. She didn't want to become part of their extended family. But it was too late for that.

There was nothing left for her except to try to find out her answers while keeping her secret.

In the bedroom she'd felt peace and pride, but not homecoming. She'd wanted to feel it, wanted a small part of the parents she'd been taken from. But it wasn't there. And then Owen had turned her into his arms. His mouth tantalized her, spoke in such a language that she was denied anything except answering. Her head and heart had separated, due to some sorcerous trick of the emotions.

And she'd been right there with him, her arms around him, her body aligned to his, her mouth fused in a kiss that should be against the law. And with a man who didn't take women seriously, a man she would never choose to pursue.

But wasn't that exactly what she was doing?

Chapter Five

Owen stared at the photograph. He'd been staring at it all night—or most of the night. Cynthia Clayton. She was smiling, looking up, her arm raised in a wave, as if she'd just seen someone she knew. She was beautiful. Owen couldn't help acknowledging that. But his gut churned.

It was too easy. No sooner had they discovered she existed than she was staring at him from the page of an eight-by-ten full-color glossy. And he knew who she was. Hell he'd already met her. Kissed her. The whole family had seen her. But he'd danced with her, invited her into his house, a place he had never brought any woman. At least not since he'd left his teenage years and his parents no longer insisted on meeting his friends.

This was too much for comfort. Owen shook his head. She had to know something, want something. Owen didn't know what, but he was determined to find out.

And he knew exactly where to start.

Owen wanted to confront Stephanie immediately, but he couldn't. Mariette was waiting for him. He was taking her shopping at a local mall. She could go alone and had been getting out on her own more. She did her own grocery shopping and made short trips to local shopping centers and nurseries for plants. Yet she still had a problem navigating the vastness of Dallas by herself.

Even though Owen had introduced her to people and she'd made some friends on her own, she was concerned about the way she looked. She'd been beaten and deformed by the mad man who'd kidnapped her and held her prisoner. The ordeal that took her away from her children for twenty years, made her shy of strangers. She seemed to enjoy the time she spent with Owen and he enjoyed being with her too. Never thinking he would again form a relationship with the woman who'd given him life, Owen had no choice but to let the anger in him go when he learned of her fate. And that she never left him and his brother by choice.

"We found her," he told Mariette as they walked toward the elevator in the Galleria.

"Cynthia?"

"The name she uses is Stephanie Hunter."

"Owen, that's wonderful," Mariette said. "But it seems fast for someone who's been missing for over thirty years."

Mariette may have been thinking of her own lengthy period of discovery.

"She registered herself at the Adoption Registry Center. The investigator we hired checked there first."

"Have you contacted her?" They went into one of the anchor department stores. Mariette stopped at one of the perfume counters inside.

"Not yet. I'm going to see her this afternoon."

His biological mother stopped and turned to

him. "Owen, you'll keep your temper." It was both a question and a request.

"I'm be more than charming," he said.

Clare hadn't been working her good luck for him in the last twenty-four hours. Owen rubbed the statue's head as he came down the stairs. He'd thought she was sending her signals his way when Stephanie was in the house, only to find out hours later that it was all a sham.

Since he'd been up all night and been out early with Mariette, Owen opened the door to go to the mailbox and pick up yesterday's mail. A messenger's envelope fell inward. Picking it up, he saw it was addressed to his mother and dropped it on the table. Someone else he would have to notify that Devon Clayton had passed away.

The mailbox held the normal daily supply of supermarket sale flyers, bills and offers for credit cards, roof repair, insurance supplements and the like. Most of it addressed to his mother. Eventually, they would stop coming, Owen thought. He sorted through the pile each night and dropped them in the shredder or the recycle bin. With these he would do the same.

He came back inside, leaving the unopened mail in its usual place, and went to make coffee. Competent in the kitchen, Owen cooked himself a hearty breakfast. He hadn't done it in months. When Dean was home or Rosa popped in for a visit they'd spend an hour or so over the meal talking and catching up. Alone he often settled for coffee and toast or picked something up on his way to the construction site or the office.

Owen wouldn't characterize himself as one of the great thinkers of the century. When he died he'd leave behind a legacy of structures that spoke of his vision of space, light, and the formation of building materials into arches, squares, triangles, and polygons. He believed some forces of nature occurred randomly, like the uniqueness of striations and colors in different granite pieces. Some were man-made, such as the metallurgical strength of an I-beam. Others had a definite pattern associated with them. Patterns like the layout of mosaic tiles or the balancing of windows on a building. When a pattern was detected the element of randomness was lost. And so it was with coincidence.

Stephanie Hunter had appeared in his life as a random encounter, an unexpected introduction based on mutual friends and allied business practices. But now Owen suspected there was no randomness to her appearance. Had she engineered it, insinuated herself into his life and that of his family with a finesse so smooth he hadn't noticed her method and he was the king of finesse?

He set the breakfast on the table, complete with silverware, jam for his toast, fried bacon, scrambled eggs, and a tall stack of pancakes. He dug in hoping the food would satisfy his anger, but it didn't. He remembered Stephanie sitting in the chair next to him just a few days ago. Her phone call and volunteering to come by could have been a plot to get into the house. She'd spent long minutes looking at the photos in the living room. She'd been holding that of his parents when he came in. Had she wanted to know what they looked like? Was that the real reason she had come?

And he'd fallen right into her trap, offering to give her the tour to keep her there for a few minutes longer. He thought he was in control, that he was directing her, turning her into his arms and kissing her with a passion he couldn't control, when all the while she was leading him by his nose.

That was about to stop.

Owen cleared the table. He'd eaten his food as nourishment. The appreciation of it was missing. Cleaning the dishes and putting them in the dishwasher reminded him of Stephanie. She was here in the house and each time Owen did anything he remembered that she had been there. He thought of how the light hit her face or shone on her hair as she sat in the kitchen, the way she smiled in Brad's room looking at his trophies, how she refused to cross the threshold of the room where he slept. And how she felt soft and boneless as he held her in his arms.

Closing the dishwasher, Owen mentally shook the image out of his head. He gathered his keys and headed for the door. He had an appointment with Ms. Hunter. She didn't know it, but she was about to see him and get some very interesting news.

He turned back, remembering the file that Simon had left with him. It was on the table with the mail. He retrieved it, noticing the envelope that had fallen inside the door. The name of a law firm showed through the plastic covering. Someone named Mary Berman of Frankel, Williams and Williams had sent the letter.

Turning the large envelope over, Owen ripped the paper strip and opened it. He pulled out a letter. As he read the air left his lungs.

Cynthia Clayton had a bank account.

Owen drove to the West Holiday shopping and office complex. He wondered who she knew to get an address in this area. This was definitely a high-rent district. She was an ingenuous woman, he thought. She'd snowed Olivia Shulman—not an easy feat—and she'd almost pulled the wool over his eyes. Just what *was* her game?

Stephanie was opening the door to her SUV when Owen pulled into the parking space next to her. He got out quickly.

"Stephanie."

She turned. Her face lit up when she saw him. Owen's stomach contracted. He wanted to rush to her and enfold her in his arms, but his mind told him he was here for another reason.

"Owen, what are you doing here?"

Since he'd met her she'd had the ability to touch his nerves and put them slightly out of place. Even now, when anger was foremost in his mind, he still felt the stirring of need for her.

"I have to talk to you."

She checked her watch. "I'm afraid it will have to wait. I have a very important appointment and I'm going to be in the middle of afternoon traffic. If I don't leave now, I'm won't make it on time."

She gave him a wink and stepped up onto the running board.

"It's about my mother."

She stopped. For a moment she seemed suspended in place, her leg bent, foot in the air, unsure if she should sit or turn back. Then she stepped down and turned to him. Her face was still, mask-like.

"Owen, I know this is the wrong place and the wrong time. I really do have an appointment and I must leave. Please meet me later and we'll talk about this?"

"I want to talk now. There's something you may not know about my parents."

"Owen." She dropped her head and folded her hands together, her thumb nervously scraping across her palm. He thought she was gathering herself for something heavy to hit her. She lifted her eyes and spoke. "Although your bloodline and mine do not mix, I know Devon and Reuben Clayton were my parents, too."

The words were calmly delivered, but they struck him like a steel beam passing through his head. He stepped back. She did know. Owen was stunned. For a moment he couldn't move. He was trying to process the information. He'd been suspicious of her, but he wanted to believe she didn't know. But she did. Of course, she knew. She'd registered Cynthia Clayton with the adoption center and left her name. Owen was obviously *not* thinking logically. When he was ready to speak again, Stephanie was pulling out of the parking space.

"Owen," she called after she'd turned the utility vehicle and pointed it toward the exit. "I'll call you tonight. We'll talk then."

With that she was gone, leaving him alone to cope with this new knowledge. Helplessly he watched her leave. Then, without a thought he began to move. Jumping into his car, he pulled into traffic several car-lengths behind her. She was heading toward downtown, exactly the area he'd just come from. Owen stayed a reasonable distance back. He wondered where she was going. When she turned onto Graham Terrace he had an aha moment. He knew she was headed for the offices of Frankel, Williams and Williams, his parents' lawyer. He had gone there first, needing to find out more about this account. Her direction nailed her as the gold digger type. She knew about the inheritance. She'd been playing him. Anger boiled in his mind. But she passed the offices and turned left at the end of the block.

Owen got to the intersection in time to see her stop at the parking lot guardhouse for Mercury

Cable, the local cable television station which comprised the next block. A moment later the bar went up and she passed through the checkpoint. She hadn't gone to the customer lot, but the private one. The lot for employees, VIPs, and guests of the station. She had to be expected. He pulled into a space in the visitors lot, feeling like a stalker waiting for his prey to emerge.

This was never going to work. It was her first time before the cameras. Why had Owen chosen today to show up? She knew by the look on his face that he was about to tell her about her parents. She'd known for a good while now. What difference could another few hours make? She needed this job. It paid well and it showcased her business.

Her own cable show on Design TV. She'd submitted the proposal tape a year ago and things were finally falling into place. She'd auditioned, shown her ideas for *Interior Design* and they'd taken it. She had a thirteen-week contract to fulfill. There was an option for more, but Stephanie didn't hold out that she'd be phenomenal enough to come back. The public was fickle and always wanted something new. But she thought it was enough time to make herself known to people who could use her services. She couldn't advertise her business on the air, but she got to plug the show's Web site, which provided a link to hers.

"We're ready, Ms. Hunter."

Stephanie took a deep breath, smiled into the camera and spoke. "Hello, and welcome to our first show. I'm Stephanie Hunter and *this* is *Interior Design*."

* * *

The taping took longer than she'd anticipated. Done in front of a live audience who didn't seem to mind having things repeated several times and a director who was patient and understanding, only made her more nervous. It took five hours for something that should have been done in two. They assured her things would go better next time. It was normal to be nervous the first day.

Stephanie knew that wasn't the reason. Owen Clayton had stepped in her calm world and destroyed her sanity. Why had he shown up at the time she was scheduled to go before a live audience and rolling cameras for the first time in her life?

Stephanie needed a drink. She wasn't a drinker, but today had been more traumatic than she'd thought it would be. She felt drained. Deciding to skip going to the office, she used her cell phone to call Owen. The secretary at his office said he hadn't been in today. At his home office she got the answering machine. She knew the house number and tried that, too. It must have been Dean's voice on the machine for it was young and happy sounding.

She left a number for Owen to return the call when he got in. By midnight she was still waiting. And it was driving her crazy. She'd spent time working on her proposal. She'd wanted to pour her heart into it, make it the best work she could possibly do. She wanted a three-dimensional mockup, but the loss of time at the studio and more time pacing as she waited for Owen to call had sapped her of energy.

Taking a last look at her proposal, Stephanie found her eyes blurring and her head pounding. She needed a break. Getting up she stretched and looked at the clock. It was twelve-thirty. She knew she'd be up the rest of the night. She grabbed a bottle of water from the refrigerator and downed it along with two aspirin. She wasn't hungry, although a big bowl of ice cream would go a long way toward appeasing her restlessness. She counted herself lucky there was none in the house.

Checking the clock in the kitchen, she noted the time and she also knew the local grocery store was open twenty-four hours. Decision made, moments later she drove out of the underground parking garage, but instead of heading for the food store she passed it and drove straight to Owen Clayton's house. Only one light was burning in an upstairs window. She recognized it as the bedroom he slept in.

Refusing to give herself time to think about what she was doing, she opened the car door and got out. Her running shoes made a soft sound on the concrete walkway. She rang the bell, pushing it hard and confidently. And that was where her confidence left her. Suddenly she wanted to flee, run back to her Firebird and drive away from this address.

She jumped when a light went on in the hall, illuminating the oval glass in the front door at the same time as the one over her head. Owen opened the door a moment later. Stephanie pushed passed him and walked into the foyer. He'd refused to call her, but she wasn't going to give him the chance to slam the door in her face.

"You could have called me back," she attacked.

"And you could have told me the truth from the first. Obviously you knew all about us before we ever knew anything about you."

Owen closed the door and they walked to the living room. "Can I get you something to drink?"

"I don't want anything to drink." She paced about the room, unable to sit down and unsure of what she was going to say to him. "I want some ice cream." It was the first thing she thought of. "I went out to get some and found myself here."

Without a word he left her. Stephanie thought she was being dismissed. Anger coiling inside her. She followed him. In the kitchen he had a container of Rocky Road ice cream on the counter and was reaching for a bowl from the cabinet. Stephanie stopped at the door when she saw what he was doing.

"Owen, I didn't know about her until a few days before your brother's wedding."

Owen said nothing. He put three scoops in the bowl and pushed it across the counter in front of the same stool where she'd sat before. Stephanie didn't want to sit down. She was much more comfortable standing. But she'd told him she wanted the ice cream.

"Aren't you going to have any?"

"No," he said, the single word making the statement as lofty and long as *War and Peace*. Stephanie grabbed the bowl and held it to her as if it could protect her from the piercing eyes of Owen Clayton.

She ate a spoonful and walked to the table, the place farthest from Owen, and sat down. "When I was sixteen years old, I found out I was adopted," she began. He listened carefully, without interruption, maintaining his position on one side of the counter, until the bowl was empty and she'd told him the whole story.

"Why didn't you tell us?"

"The timing was wrong. First the wedding, the wrong place to have a scene. Then after the funeral it wasn't time for a long-lost relative to come waltzing through he door. You'd all think I was a gold digger or something."

"What did you want us to think?"

"Nothing," she shouted. "I wasn't there for you. I'd barely learned of your existence." She meant the entire Clayton Clan. Stephanie stood up. While she left the safety of the table, she didn't approach Owen. "You're adopted. You must know what it's like to want to know who your birth parents are."

"I do know who they are."

"Then you know what your life would be like if you'd grown up with them." She saw the almost imperceptible stiffening of his arms. "I wanted that. My aunt and uncle kept it a secret. Of course, I know why now. You don't broadcast a kidnapping. But I wanted to learn what I could about the one living parent I still had."

"And that's why you came to the hospital?"

Stephanie nodded. "I wondered if she'd know me. If there was any connection between parent and child that even time couldn't destroy. I never got to find out."

"There is."

Stephanie's head came up and she stared at him. "What do you mean?"

"She made me promise to find you."

"How?"

"She must have recognized something in you. While she was lying on the floor in that bathroom and you were slipping out the door, she gripped my arm and using what breath she had, told me to *find Cynthia*."

Stephanie stepped back, bumping into a chair.

"So what now, *Cynthia*?" Owen's voice was angry. "What do you want?"

"Nothing." She flashed angry eyes at him.

"Nothing?" he shouted. "The will divides everything among her children. That would include you." Finally he moved. He took a step toward her and Stephanie wanted to run, but she couldn't move.

"I'm not here for money."

"Aren't you? You want me to believe you're just a little lost waif who wanted to find her parents?"

"It's the truth." Stephanie stood up straight.

He kept taking steps toward her. Each one punctuated his words. "Of course, there will be tests required. After all, we can't just take *your* word that you're Cynthia Clayton."

"I don't give a damn what you think," she shouted. "I have never been Cynthia Clayton that I can remember. My name is Stephanie Hunter." She paused to let it sink in. "And you can keep your mother's will exactly as it stands. Without me."

Turning on the balls of her feet, she whipped her hair across her shoulders and headed for the door.

"Stephanie," Owen called before she got there. She stopped, but continued to face her escape route.

"Is this what you do when you're angry? Eat ice cream?"

The video conferencing equipment Dean had insisted everyone get and set up had only been used once for a family conference. Owen knew several family members would get together and use it to talk face-to-face, but tonight would be the second time they had an electronic family meeting and the first time he'd called for it.

After Stephanie left, he'd sent E-mails to the

other Claytons announcing the meeting. He needed to let them know about Cynthia, that not only had she been found, but that they all had at least seen her once.

"Hi, Owen," Erin said happily as she and Digger appeared on the screen.

"Hi." He tried to smile, but was sure it didn't come across. His sisters-in-law, both Mallory and Erin, were quick to read his moods.

"We got the pictures you sent." He'd sent them the scanned photo of Cynthia that the private investigator had left with him.

"Hi." Dean and Rosa came on at the same time. Then Luanne and her husband Mark Rogers arrived. By the appointed time all six of the Clayton children and their related spouses were present, each appearing as a small square on the big screen. Owen adjusted the size so each screen was the same size and the block of them filled the entire fifty inches.

For a few moments they asked about other family members, children, mutual friends. Then it seemed by common agreement they quieted for the business at hand.

"What's up, Owen?" Dean asked. "You've got that look of doom on your face."

Owen tried to change his expression. "You all have the photo?"

Several of them had printed it and were looking at it from their rooms across the globe. Rosa was in Italy and had hooked up her equipment in a hotel conference room. People of Rosa's stature and her smile got her what she wanted. Owen looked at the picture of Stephanie and quickly looked away. She was a gold digger, he told himself. Despite what she said, he believed her appearance at the crucial time had been more than coincidental.

"This is Cynthia Clayton."

"Are you sure?" Erin asked. "Isn't this the woman from the museum?"

"What museum?" Brad asked.

"The Women's Museum. We were there for an opening a few days ago. She was there," Owen explained.

"She even sat our table, talked to us," Rosa said, not even trying to disguise her sarcasm.

"She's about to begin a show on Design TV," Erin informed them. "There's an article on her in one of my magazines."

"I've seen her before, too," Mallory said.

"We all have," Owen explained. "She was the woman at the reception who saved Mother's life." For a moment there was silence. "I also saw her at the burial."

"I did, too," Dean said as if he were remembering the day or perhaps passing her as he went out the front door of their home.

"The name she's using is Stephanie Hunter," Owen supplied.

"I didn't expect Thalberg would find her so quickly," Brad said. Owen knew he was thinking of the years it had taken to find his and Brad's biological mother. It seemed unfair that Cynthia Clayton could be found with so little time and effort.

"Apparently, she had been looking for us."

"For us," Rosa said.

"Not *us*. The Claytons. She'd been to the National Registry of Adopted Children and registered herself."

"As Cynthia Clayton?" Rosa asked.

Owen nodded. "She was looking for the parents of Cynthia Clayton. She left her name as Stephanie Hunter."

"Have you talked to her?" Luanne asked.

Owen nodded and dropped his head. He didn't want anything to show on his face. He'd done more than talk to her. He'd kissed her, felt her long legs down the length of his own. He could taste her on his lips and he felt arousal tighten his body at the thought.

"What did she have to say?" Brad asked.

He related the story as quickly as he could, leaving nothing out, except that the conversation had taken place less than twenty-four hours ago, in the kitchen of the house where they'd all grown up.

"What do you think we should do now?" Digger asked.

Owen waited for someone else to answer. They were all quiet, as if finding her had been the end of the cycle. Now that a real person existed, someone whom they'd met, someone made of flesh and blood, no longer a face on a yellowed newspaper clipping with fold lines through her cherubic smile, they had no further plans.

"Owen, you say she lives in Dallas?" Luanne asked.

"Yes," he replied.

"I suppose if we all descend on her it will scare her to death."

"She said she was looking for her family," Rosa replied. "We're it. Take us or leave us."

Owen watched as Erin and Mallory smiled at the comment. His youngest sister was always straight to the point.

"There's something I'd like to investigate before we make any plans," Owen told them.

"What is it?" Dean asked.

Owen took a deep breath. "Yesterday I had an appointment with Joseph Frankel of Frankel, Williams and Williams."

"Sounds like a law firm," Brad stated.

"It is. They were retained by Mom and Dad years ago, before any of us came into their lives."

"They knew about Cynthia?" Brad asked, but his question had the finality of a statement.

"Mr. Frankel is retired now and has been on an extended vacation out of the country. Most of his papers were packed up years ago and his cases passed to a younger member of the staff."

"Except for the one that got lost and has just been found." Dean recited the sentence as if it were a treatment for a potential movie idea.

"The file contained some legal papers and a bank account."

"Bank account?" Dean spoke.

"In the name of Cynthia Clayton."

"Wouldn't it be dormant by now?" Digger asked.

"As long as the statements go to an address and are not returned, an account remains active. Periodically, an audit letter is mailed to confirm the account's validity. Apparently Frankel's secretary had been performing this function. When she left the firm, she turned over the responsibility to a young woman named Mary Berman who didn't question why she was doing it, only that it was part of the procedure. All the interest on the account has been reinvested in it."

"How much money is in this account?" Luanne asked.

Owen hesitated, looking at the individual blocks on the television monitor in one of the upstairs bedrooms.

"Four million dollars."

"What?" Luanne said.

"According to Mr. Frankel, when Cynthia was kidnapped the story went out in newspapers and Mom and Dad made a plea on television for her return. People began sending letters and money. They assumed there was a ransom that needed to be paid. Much of the money came anonymously and couldn't be returned. So they set up an account for her. When she wasn't returned, Mr. Frankel suggested they use it as a retirement fund. Both said they would think about it, but never made a decision. It's been sitting there compounding interest for the last thirty-four years."

"How did you find out about the account?" Digger asked.

"Mom is still getting mail. A letter came addressed to her from this law office. Apparently when Joseph Frankel returned for a visit to the firm he saw the bank statement. He suggested someone send a letter with options for investing the money."

"Is this what you want to investigate?" Brad asked.

"I want to find out if Stephanie Hunter is telling the truth—if she's who she claims to be."

"A simple DNA test can tell you that," Brad stated. "All you need is a sample of her blood or a swab from her mouth."

"How about a bowl of ice cream?"

Brad and Mallory, both doctors, exchanged glances, but nodded that it could be done.

"I also want to know if she somehow knows about the money."

"And then what?" Dean asked.

"We'll have another meeting after that and decide a course of action."

He saw nods from most of the family. After a few more minutes of surprise and speculation, they signed off. Dean was the last on the screen when everyone else was gone.

"Owen?" he called.

"Yes."

"She was coming in as I left."

It wasn't a question, but he answered it anyway. "Yes."

"How is it going?"

"What do you mean?"

"I mean you've never invited a woman to our house before. Is there something between the two of you?"

"She came by to pick up some papers. She's bidding on the *Dallas Herald*."

"And you made lunch for a business acquaintance? What? Did Jake's go out of business?" Dean's voice and face showed his skeptical acceptance of Owen's replies.

"Tell me, are you really all right?"

Owen looked him straight in the eye. "Of course."

Dean waited without comment for a moment. Owen and Dean shared the house when Dean was in town and they'd grown close enough to read each other's moods.

"You're falling for her, aren't you?"

Owen put on his best face—at least the one he thought gave nothing away. "You know me, Dean. No one woman is as good as many women."

"But this one is different," he stated.

Owen thought about Stephanie. She'd occupied more of his mind than other women. He liked talking to her. He certainly liked having her in his arms. And since he'd met her, he hadn't been interested in any other woman. Was he falling for her? Was that the reason finding out she was Cynthia had so angered him? He didn't know and wouldn't commit to anything. His trust of the opposite sex was low. And she was proving his rule. She was as untrustworthy as any of her sex where he was concerned. Brad and Digger had found their life mates. Luanne was as much in love with Mark today as she'd been when they married. Yet Owen never expected to find a woman who'd prove anything more than a showpiece.

And that included Stephanie Hunter *and* Cynthia Clayton. But he admitted to Dean. "She is different."

The mind is truly a wonderfully resilient organ, Stephanie thought. She curled mascara on her eyelashes in the bathroom mirror. With her going crazy over what Owen must think of her after their argument, getting that proposal in on time, taping her programs at Design TV, and maintaining her business, she should have lost her mind by now. Actually, she was grateful for the distractions. She didn't know what she would have done had it not been for the busy-ness of her life.

And Emilie.

Returning to the bedroom, Stephanie grabbed the short yellow jacket that complemented her tightly beaded tube-top and slipped it around her shoulders. She was meeting Emilie for dinner, an event she didn't want to attend, but her friend insisted that sitting home moping was not healthy. There was a new man in Emilie's life and tonight Stephanie would meet him.

Psychologically adjusting her attitude and thinking of something happy, she smiled and relaxed her shoulders. Adding earrings and a necklace as final touches, she left the room and headed for the apartment door. Pulling it open, she found Owen about to knock. He took an awkward step forward, but maintained his balance. Stephanie, surprised at his appearance, stumbled back as the need to put distance between them seemed apparent.

"I guess I should have called," he stated. His eyes looked her up and down. Stephanie knew yellow was a good color for her. Yet under her skin she could feel the color spreading into her face and painting it a deeper shade of red.

"Yes, you should have," Stephanie agreed. She was both relieved and apprehensive at seeing him. Other than the tone of his voice, she wasn't about to let him know his unexpected appearance jangled her nerves. Her stomach fell and her breath caught in her throat, but she stood straight and kept her expression calm. Why did he have to be so good-looking? Then she told herself he had a reputation that included a harem of women. She was not going to join the ensemble. "Did you want something?"

"Do we have to discuss it at the door?"

"I'm on my way out." Suddenly she was afraid of whatever he had to tell her and she didn't want him in her apartment, didn't want the memory of his presence when she came in at night or woke in the morning. "I'm meeting a friend for dinner."

"I haven't eaten. I'll come with you. We can talk on the way." Before Stephanie could refuse, he'd taken her arm and pulled her into the hallway.

She freed herself. "How do you know my friend isn't a man?"

He stammered. Clearly the thought had not occurred to him and this made her angry. "Is he?"

"Yes," she said, then dropped her head. "Actually, it's my friend Emilie and her new boyfriend, but you didn't know that."

"You didn't know if I was alone a few nights ago, either."

Her head came up quickly. She hadn't considered it and she should have. "I apologize," she said after a moment.

Owen smiled. "Do you think Emilie and her new boyfriend will mind if I join you for dinner?" He paused. "Or do *you* mind?"

"The last time we were together we had a very heated . . . discussion. Would you want to continue that in front of total strangers?" She searched his face intently for a reaction. He gave her none. "You must have made a decision on the new knowledge you acquired since that night."

"I have."

She waited for him to continue. "Are you going to tell me what it is?" she asked.

"I've decided yours is the best design and the most financially feasible. If you want it, the contract is yours."

Stephanie was so stunned, she nearly took a step back. "What?" she said.

"The design contract for the *Dallas Herald*. It's yours. The design was not only better than any of the others, but providing a three-dimensional representation of the entrance and major work areas was a brilliant aid in translating the flat two-dimensional boards to something more ecstatically pleasing. Once the committee looked at your bid it tipped the scales in your favor."

"Thank you," she mumbled. Stephanie should be pleased, doing the Snoopy dance or turning cartwheels down the hall, but he'd taken the joy out of the award. She'd spent a couple of days and nights on that proposal, using her sewing and limited crafting skills to put together a representation of what she didn't have time to put on paper. But that shouldn't be the subject of discussion. Owen was talking about a contract when she'd told him his adoptive mother was her real mother. How could he come here to give her a contract when there was a more important subject between them.

"Stop it!" she shouted. "I'm serious and you're trying to make light of it."

His face, which had been serious, turned grave before her. "This is not a light decision. I spent days going through the proposals and yours is the best; but if you don't—"

"That's not it," she interrupted a little too quickly. "I'm glad, thrilled, exhilaratingly ecstatic to be chosen" —her hands were in the air emphasizing her delight— "but is this the real reason you appear on my doorstep unannounced? You could have phoned my office or responded by mail as the instructions stated would be the method of communication. Yet, you're here." She consulted her watch. "At seven-thirty at night, unexpected. There must be some other reason."

Stephanie pulled the door closed behind her and they walked toward the elevator. Her heels made no noise on the carpeted floor. Owen stopped, taking her arm and drawing her around to face him. "I want to know who you are. I thought if we spent some time together we could get to know each other," he said.

"And why would you want to do that?" Stephanie was skeptical and made no effort to hide it.

"For many reasons. The Claytons were my parents. They never told us about you. I want to know why."

"And the DNA thing?" Stephanie didn't quite believe him. It was a good argument and she knew she was attracted to him, that she wanted to know more about him and his family, but she was used to people keeping secrets from her when it came to the history of her birth.

"There is that." He dropped his arms and looked uncomfortable when he said it. Stephanie's heart softened. They resumed walking. Stephanie pushed the button to call the elevator. She stole a glance in Owen's direction. It was time to deliver another bombshell and she might as well do it now.

The elevator door slid into the recessed pocket and she stepped inside. "I've already had the test and the results," she said. As expected he stopped on the outside of the small room as if a glass wall prevented him from crossing the threshold.

"You've already had the test?"

The door started to close. Owen remained stationary for a moment. Neither of them reached out to stop it until it had nearly reached its closed position. Then Owen's arm snapped through the opening and the reflective door retracted. His face was thunderous when he came into view again.

"You've already had the test?" he repeated. "How? How could you get the comparison records? Medical reports are confidential."

"I didn't need medical records." The door closed and the descent was quick. She got out as soon as it opened enough to accommodate her width. Taking a deep breath she headed for the exit. The lobby had a security guard sitting inside a circular desk that contained a series of television monitors. Stephanie nodded to him. He always announced unexpected guests. Where had he been when Owen arrived?

Owen touched her elbow as they approached the front door. Feeling as if a hot electric current passed up her arm, Stephanie stepped away from him. "I'd better drive," she said and crossed to the elevators that ascended to the building's parking garages.

"Are you going to answer my question?" Owen asked when Stephanie was weaving through the streets of Dallas.

After a moment, Stephanie began to talk. "You were adopted, Owen, so you might understand the overwhelming force to know about your past. Your adoption came after you knew your parents, but you're only slightly different from me. I knew nothing. For years I wondered who my parents were. Why had they given me away? You had Brad to talk to. I had no one. I wondered why my aunt disliked me so, yet doted on my brothers. Now I understand she was afraid and each time she looked at me that fear would raise its head again. When I found the papers saying I was adopted, they wouldn't talk to me about them. It was like living in a black hole."

"Until Brad's wedding?"

"A little before that." She took a moment to glance in his direction. Stephanie had the top up on her convertible, but she could see that his gaze was intense. For a moment she wished she was driving the SUV. The distance between her and Owen would be greater. In the Firebird it was like she was touching him. She wished she could. Wished that he was more easily accepting of her, but she knew she would act the same if someone had come out of the woodwork and claimed they were a family member just at the time a parent died and nothing could be verified.

Yet Stephanie had verified that Reuben and Devon Clayton *were* her biological parents.

"Go on," Owen prompted.

"After my parents died—the woman who kidnapped me and her husband," she explained. She'd never called them anything except Mom and Dad. It felt strange to refer to them as if they were criminals. "After they died, my brothers and I left St. Louis and came to live with our aunt and uncle here in Dallas. When I was sixteen and needed my birth certificate for driver's ed, I found out I'd been adopted. After that the papers disappeared and I couldn't get anymore information. I learned not to ask. A few weeks before your brother's wedding my uncle was ill and I went to see him. He's fine now, but the adoption papers were there along with newspaper clippings about Cynthia Clayton's kidnapping."

"So you assumed you and Cynthia Clayton were the same person?"

"It wasn't as cold as that. Yes, I did make the assumption, but that wasn't enough. I had to be sure."

"So as my mother lay dying, you took a blood sample?" His voice was incredulous.

"Of course I didn't," Stephanie countered.

"Well, are you going to get to the point anytime this century?"

"I thought you wanted the whole story, not the condensed version."

"I want the truth."

Stephanie sighed and continued. "The day I went to the hospital Devon was unconscious and uncomfortable. Her breathing was labored and I called the nurse. The woman turned her and she breathed easier, but she also drooled. I used the tissues in the room to soak up the wetness. Just before I left I took the soaked tissues and replaced them with dry ones."

"And realized what you were holding?"

Stephanie nodded. "I had the proof in my hands. All I needed to prove to myself that the woman lying in that bed was my mother was to compare a swab of cotton from my mouth to the tissues."

"It must have been irresistible."

Stephanie ignored his sarcasm. He was loyal to Devon Clayton. She would be, too, in his position. Her face muscles relaxed a moment. Devon would be proud of him, protecting her even in death.

"I opened the drawer and found a box of plastic gloves. I put the tissues in one of them and tied a knot to keep them moist."

"Then all you needed was a private lab and your own sample."

"Private labs are more common than they used to be and with DNA the test is simple, but I didn't use a private lab. I know people at a local hospital and I had the test run there. If the variations had been more diverse a more sophisticated lab would have been necessary."

"But your results were right on the money."

"Ninety-nine and six tenths percent." Stephanie didn't gloat over her success. She lowered her voice to a whisper. "Owen, she was my mother."

He didn't say a word, making Stephanie more nervous than if he'd continued his sarcasm.

"I had to know, as much as you want to know. You can have a DNA swab anytime you want and have your own test performed."

She pulled into the restaurant's parking lot and stopped the car. Turning to him she wanted to break the heavy air that encapsulated this speck of the universe. Releasing her seat belt, she reached over and put her hand on his arm. There was a slight tightening of the muscles under her fingers, but he did not pull away.

"Do you think we can hold off on testing until after dessert?"

Chapter Six

Dinner was an absolute disaster. A volcanic eruption in downtown Dallas would have been preferable to the conversation at the table. Emilie couldn't have been more surprised and pleased, it appeared, to see Stephanie approaching the table with Owen Clayton in tow. While Owen had been almost a statue in the car, he was animated and charming at dinner, drawing every word out of Emilie as if the emergency room nurse was saving his life by providing him with the information he needed to survive.

And she was willing to lay Stephanie's life on the table as if she were the gourmet meal. In an hour and a half, Emilie had told of their college antics, Stephanie's work with Josh, her selling her home to start her company and her garnering the contract on Design TV. The only subject she didn't bring up was Stephanie's adoption.

Stephanie was left trying to have a conversation with Emilie's date, Michael Vance, while listening with one ear to her best friend. Michael was an interesting young man. He was a pharmaceutical representative who'd once worked as a lab technician. Interested in rock climbing and skiing, he often spent time in Colorado and Wyoming.

Stephanie could only hope she was coherent when she spoke to Michael. Her mind was not on him, through no fault of his. Owen had said he wanted to get to know her. Was that what he was doing talking to Emilie? He was certainly attentive, listening to her and asking questions. The fact that Stephanie felt like a bug under a microscope didn't stop them in the least.

During the drive back to her condo, Stephanie tried to remember what she'd eaten or even if she'd eaten. The night was a jumble of stories and reactions, mostly her trying to figure out what Owen was thinking. Her head had begun to ache and she was glad she didn't have to keep up a conversation on the way home. But she wanted to know what Owen thought. What he would do next. By the time she'd parked and they got into the elevator, she was boiling over with curiosity.

"Owen, you haven't said anything about what I told you before we went to dinner. You were riveted to Emilie's stories. With what I told you, do you believe me?"

He stared at her. Stephanie tried to read what was in his eyes.

"I'm not trying to barge into your family," she continued. "That was never my intention. Devon and Reuben are gone. There is no need for me to ever see any of you again. I just want to know."

"You're willing to walk away from us?"

"Except for the commission, which I am accepting, I have no further designs on you or your family."

"I thought you wanted to know all about us."

"You are intriguing . . . I mean all of you, your

stories, how you came to be a family, how you came to live with Devon and Reuben, but we have no bloodline. I'm not your sister."

"You're damn right you're not my sister." Then he did something totally unexpected. He swept Stephanie into his arms and kissed her. She was so surprised she didn't react, but lay stiffly with her body against his without moving. Slowly she felt the pressure of his mouth combine with internal fires that had her moving her arms around his neck and joining him in the kiss.

She knew better than to let this go on. She knew he didn't believe her, that this kiss was a test, one she could fail. But she no longer cared. His mouth did wondrous things to hers, his tongue a total invasion that she accepted for the pleasure it promised.

It could have been seconds or years that he held her, that his hands rummaged in her hair, dislodging her pinned-up style and letting it flow freely over his hands and down her back. It could have been years that his mouth tantalized hers, that his breathing mingled with hers, that his caresses sent chills along her spine to dampen the heated coil generated within her. Locked together, the tiny room's heat regulator, accelerating with Stephanie's heartbeat, threatened to burst into flame as their combined heat turned them into an inferno.

Stephanie could no longer remember dinner, the conversation, meeting Michael Vance, or Emilie regaling them with her stories. She only knew Owen's mouth on hers. It was wet and hot and sensation flowed through her like hot wax. Her arms were all over Owen and his over her.

Suddenly a burst of cold air hit Stephanie from behind and the bell of the elevator snapped her back to reality. Her mind knew they were on the

ground, but not her body. That was still fused to
Owen's, soaring high above them on some celes-
tial plane. Owen held her, breathing hard in her
ear and trying to control his own erratic emotions.
She could feel his chest hard against hers.

Time passed and Stephanie pushed herself free.
Owen took a step away from her and the two
looked at each other. Neither knew what to say, yet
they both wanted to say something. Finally breath
returned to Stephanie.

"I suppose that was good-bye." She found her
voice first.

Owen's growl was deep and ragged with emotion. "Not by a long shot," he said.

The woman was messing with his head. Owen
stood looking at the FedEx envelope discarded on
his desk and the single sheet of paper bearing the
logo of Stephanie Hunter's design firm. Every day
since she'd come into his life the two of them were
engaged in some drama. He got up and looked
through the windows. Downtown Dallas was the
same. None of the buildings had imploded during
the night and neither had any new ones sprung
up, full grown and ready for occupancy without his
knowledge. Yet he'd changed, and apparently so
had Stephanie Hunter.

She was refusing the contract. Why the hell had
she said she wanted it? She'd obviously spent days
on the proposal and she'd accepted it a week ago
in the confines of a very hot elevator. Now she was
formally withdrawing her bid. He knew the *Dallas
Herald* was the largest commission she'd ever received.

So why was she throwing it aside like dirty bath
water? It had to have something to do with him.

He shouldn't have kissed her in that elevator, but he couldn't control it. When she opened the door to her apartment earlier that evening he'd thought he was prepared to see her, but he wasn't. Unlike any other woman he'd ever known, she surprised him each time he saw her. And this time she bowled him over. She was going out, dressed for a date. Her hair was up again, not braided as it had been when he'd first seen her, but styled in a way that made him want to run his fingers through it. Her suit was yellow with a strapless top that offered viewing to a lot of skin and drew the eye to her neckline where the promise of cleavage was more than apparent. Her eye shadow was two-toned, light and dark brown, and when combined with eyelashes as long as fringe, the total effect was dramatic. Who was she going to see dressed like that?

He looked back at the envelope. It wasn't nepotism, he thought. Stephanie *was* qualified for the job. He wouldn't bend his standards to keep an eye on her, although he did want her within reach to find out her true motive for seeking out the Claytons. He didn't for one second believe that she was only seeking her roots.

He'd spent a lifetime not worrying about his, but his brother Brad had never let go of the dream of finding their biological mother. And through Brad's efforts they had found her. Stephanie could have mounted the same kind of campaign to find them.

Owen sat down in his big comfortable leather chair. His office was in Fountain Place, looking out on a vista of tall buildings that rolled away to a serene scene of sun-scorched earth.

Punching a button on his phone, he got an outside line and started to dial Stephanie's office when the buzz from his secretary interrupted him.

"Ellen, get me Stephanie Hunter on the phone." He didn't wait for her to tell him why she buzzed.

"She's here. She doesn't have an appointment, but wants to see you."

"Here?"

"Yes." Ellen sounded confused. "Shall I show her in?"

In seconds Owen put down the phone and opened the door. She was wearing a pink suit. The jacket was short, stopping at her waist and the back flared out in neat columns of pleats that graduated in length, forming a point in the center. Her skirt, shoes, and purse were the same pink color. Only the black briefcase hanging from her arm interrupted the color scheme. She must have known pink was a good color on her, for she was striking as she stood there.

"Please, come in," he invited, showing none of the discomfort she afforded him whenever she was near. "This is a surprise," he said when she was seated before his desk and he'd resumed his chair.

"I apologize for not calling, but after I mailed the letter I remembered you delivered your offer in person. It's only reasonable that I should refuse it in the same manner."

"I don't understand." He steepled his fingers and stared at her.

"I've come for my mock-up." He looked at the large square table that housed drawers on two sides to hold blueprints. The top surface held her rendering of proposed plans for the interior. Stephanie followed his gaze. She got up and walked to it, looking at the offices, the color schemes, the reception area with its unique chandelier made of retooled parts from old printing presses. It even lighted up when a switch was thrown, activating a small battery. Alongside it were the other five proposals he'd considered before choosing hers.

"I don't understand your decision." He joined her in front of her rendering. The sun shone on her hair, which was coiled into a French roll. Owen remembered threading his fingers through the mass and pocketed them to keep them from doing it again.

"Like I said in the letter, I can't take on a job of this magnitude right now."

"You were not of that opinion a week ago."

She faced him, but moved around the display keeping distance between them. Owen wondered if she sensed his earlier thoughts.

"Isn't this the largest commission you've received?" he asked, knowing the answer.

"Yes," she confirmed with honesty. She looked him directly in the eye when she said it.

He picked up one of the rejected proposals and opened it, sitting it like a stand-up book on the free section of the table. Flipping the pages he showed her the proposal. Then doing the same with the others, he could see that hers was clearly the best.

"If you think I chose yours out of some sort of family loyalty, you're wrong."

"That's not it."

"Then what is it? This job could put you on the map." She said nothing. "Talk to me." He took a step toward her and she immediately retreated. "It's me? You can't work with me?"

She nodded.

"Why not?"

"Owen, every time I'm around you I end up in your arms. That won't be good for my career and it inevitably happens. People will notice and that will be worse for my career than if I don't accept the job."

"I see." His body was tense. He made no effort to relax it. "Well, I can't very well not work on my own project."

"I understand. I'll be going. I'm sure any one of the other designers will do an acceptable job."

She reached for the rendering. Through a method of hinges and slip locks the entire unit would fold up into the size of a small suitcase. Owen moved across the room and stopped her by putting his hand on it.

"Adequate, but not superb, not the best it can be. And I need it to be the best."

"Thank you."

"That wasn't a compliment. This is a business proposal. You do your job. I'll do mine, and the two of us need only discuss the business. Deal?" He stepped away from her, raising his hands in the air. "No hands."

Stephanie hesitated. He wanted her around, true, because he couldn't get enough of looking at her and wanting her, but also because her design was the best he'd seen in years. She knew what the owners wanted. Her questions were more to their needs than an array of complementing colors. Maybe it was the newness of her business, the need to succeed, or a desire to change the tried and true to something different, but she had an eye for it that appealed to him and would appeal to his clients.

In the few days she'd had to produce the proposal, along with the turmoil of knowing their two families converged, she'd interviewed some of the people who would occupy the space, read Internet articles on others to get a feel for their likes and dislikes. She wasn't interested in making it another office building with soothing and work-inducing colors. Stephanie's proposal showed concern for body esthetics, intelligent lighting, and comfort. Her written text had mentioned the number of hours people would spend in these surroundings and the amount of comfort they needed to complete jobs on time.

She'd suggested a break room with light, stress-relieving equipment and possibly a full-time back and neck massage therapist. Owen had taken the liberty of suggesting this to the owners, using her arguments. Even though the building would have a full gym and exercise room in the basement, often people needed just a few minutes to unwind before returning to computers that could be a health hazard as well as a godsend. The owners had readily accepted her idea and Owen was amending the design to incorporate it.

"All right," Owen began after formulating an argument. "I'll tell you a secret. An architect is only as good as his last design. The fact is, this is a very important project for me and I need you and your design." It was the truth, but he also needed to keep tabs on her for the family. Putting that argument aside for the moment, he continued. "I give you free hand to do the designs as you've outlined them and they've been accepted. Any changes need to be discussed with me. You can do it by phone, E-mail, fax or carrier pigeon if seeing me is such a chore." He waited for her to frown, but she kept her face annoyingly serene and inflexibly beautiful.

"Go on."

"You stay strictly within budget. Any variations need approval."

She nodded.

"And while you're working on site, I will be working somewhere else. Is that acceptable?"

He waited for her to answer. He almost held his breath, wanting her to accept, but unsure of her reply. For the longest moment he wondered what she would say. She needed the money for her business and she needed the prestige this job would give her. He had her in a corner. Yet she seemed to be weighing the idea. And it pissed him off to think that she didn't want him around. Who did she think she was? A queen? He had women falling over themselves to get a chance with him. But this one was different. This one mattered?

"Is it a deal?"

"Deal," she said.

Owen offered his hand. Stephanie took several steps to place hers in it. Unexpectedly, his hand tingled. He felt that more than a handshake was going on. If she hadn't gotten into his blood already, she was doing it now. Like the victim in an old horror movie, he welcomed the transformation.

Marian Morton graduated from design school the previous May. She answered a short ad Stephanie posted on an electronic board for design students. After a short interview, Stephanie hired her. She liked the young woman immediately and thought she would add something to the firm that was suddenly being overwhelmed with requests. Marian quickly proved her worth. Not only was she organized, but she had a sharp memory and a creative mind that looked at the world in terms of texture, color, and form. She was exactly what Stephanie was looking for in an assistant.

With Marian working on the design of the office

complex in several departments of the news building, Stephanie was free to concentrate on the executive offices, which had to be functional, uncluttered, and visually appealing to the members of Dallas's Fourth Estate. In other words, the local newspaper empire.

Stephanie tapped her drawing pencil against the blotter on her drawing table. Her usual method would be to visit the client and find out as much about him or her that she could. She'd ask what they wanted so she could incorporate their personal preferences into the project. She wouldn't be able to do that with them just yet, but she could do the next best thing.

Two hours later, Stephanie pulled her SUV into the parking lot of Jake's. Marian was with her. Stephanie sat for a moment after cutting the engine. She remembered her last encounter at this restaurant, but put it and thoughts of Owen aside.

"Anything wrong?" Marian asked.

Stephanie turned to her and shook her head. "I was remembering being here a while ago. It wasn't the best meeting." She opened the door and stepped into the lunchtime heat.

"Mrs. Shulman," Stephanie greeted her as the maitre'd led them to the table. She stretched her hand out to the older woman who sat at the exact table where Owen had sat with Gemma Lawson. It hadn't been Stephanie's choice of an eatery, but when she'd called Olivia Shulman with her request, the woman had jumped at the idea of helping and quickly suggested they meet at Jake's.

"Please call me Olivia," she said. "I assume we're friends now."

Stephanie introduced Marian and the two shook hands.

"Have her show you my husband's offices,"

Olivia told Marian, including the new decorator in the offer of friendship. Then she turned back to Stephanie. "You wish to know something about the heads at the *Herald*?"

"Marian has found bios on them and we're trying to read between the lines. We plan to talk to them directly, but anything you can tell us about their likes and dislikes will help us present a design that they can work with. Knowing they are busy people, we don't want to waste their time with several samples of unacceptable color schemes or furniture styles."

"Pay attention, Marian. She's a very good teacher."

Olivia looked up then. She smiled and her face brightened. Stephanie turned to see who she'd seen and froze in place when the tall, dark, and handsome frame of Owen Clayton strode toward them with the sleekness of a black panther.

"I asked Owen to join us. Between the two of us you'll get more than enough information to start."

Stephanie sat still as Owen kissed Olivia's cheek and was introduced to Marian. Shaking both their hands, he slid into the seat next to Olivia and directly in front of Stephanie. Her legs suddenly felt heavy and she was extremely thirsty. Why hadn't Olivia told her she'd called Owen? He was the last person she wanted to deal with today.

"I didn't want to bother Owen," she explained to Olivia. "I know you're—"

"It's no bother," he interrupted her. "I often have lunch here."

At that moment the waiter arrived and took their drink order. Stephanie couldn't remember what she ordered the moment the man walked away. She was concentrating on Owen. He wasn't going to make this easy for her. He made her ner-

vous and he knew it. He also knew she didn't want
to be around him and he'd agreed to her terms.
Well, almost. He said he wouldn't be at the site
when she was working there. This was neutral ter-
ritory and *she* had not called him.

". . . to help you out," Owen was saying when
her attention returned. Stephanie struggled to re-
gain the thread of conversation. "I've set up ap-
pointments with Addison, Halpern and Worth."
That was John Addison, publisher; Harry Halpern,
general manager; and Seymour Worth, director of
circulation. "They can each give you an hour on
Wednesday, Thursday and Friday. Will that be
enough time?"

"Initially," she agreed. "After the meeting I'll
work up something for them to approve."

He nodded.

When the logistics were confirmed, they began
the impromptu meeting. Stephanie found her
professional front and started taking notes. Marian,
who hadn't said a word beyond hello when she was
introduced, was quite animated and interesting.
Despite the age difference, she presented herself
equal to the task. Stephanie was glad she'd hired
her. The young woman had the makings of a good
decorator.

Soon after the meal, Olivia excused herself. She
surprised Stephanie by offering Marian a ride back
to the office. This would leave Stephanie alone with
Owen. Suddenly she believed this meeting hadn't
been so impromptu. It appeared as if someone was
engineering the situation, forcing her to be in
Owen's presence.

But Stephanie had her own ace in the hole.
"That won't be necessary, Olivia," she broke in.
"We're done here. I'm on my way back to the of-
fice. Marian can ride with me."

"I'd like to talk to you for a moment," Owen said. His statement conveyed he wanted privacy. Stephanie's teeth clenched, but she was forced to agree to his plans. He was technically her boss, although she didn't feel as if they had an employer-employee relationship.

She nodded at Marian. "I can check on those fabric samples for the sound walls and call Mrs. Clayburn about her beach house," Marian pointed out the work waiting for her back at the West Holiday office.

A moment later Stephanie was alone with the man she'd told she didn't want to see just over a week ago. And one who'd filled her dreams every night since.

"Would you like something else?" he asked as if he were the waiter.

She shook her head and sipped from the glass of water on the table in front of her. She noticed him searching her face as if he were looking for some resemblance. She wondered if he was comparing her to her parents. Did he see them in her? She wanted to ask. She wanted to know what he saw when he looked at her. And she wanted to know why his eyes could cause her heart to pound wildly and her stomach to feel as if she were at the top of a roller coaster about to plunge into the abyss.

Unable to compete with his patient staring, Stephanie started the conversation. "Is it the blood you want to talk about?" She'd gone to the clinic his lawyer arranged and had the DNA swab done. Additionally, they had required a blood sample. It surprised Stephanie, but she complied with the request.

"The lab is working on the results. I'm not here

for that, however, I want to talk to you about the family."

"Your family?"

He nodded.

"What about them?"

"They want to meet you."

"What?" She was confused. She thought he wanted to ask her questions about her family.

"My brothers and sisters. They're curious, confused, unsure how to proceed. They want to meet you."

Stephanie, too, was confused. She'd wanted to meet them for years. Even not knowing they existed, she wanted to believe there was a family out there who really wanted her. She'd built fantasies in her mind like every other adopted child she'd met since discovering her own situation. She'd crashed a wedding for the chance to glimpse them and now they wanted to meet her. Fear skated up her back. She clamped down the thought that they really wanted something else.

"Why?" she asked.

"We've never had a lost sister."

"I'm not your sister."

"I stand corrected. They didn't know the parents that raised them had a child. Naturally, they want to get to know you."

He spoke in the third person, as if he was not part of the group that wanted to know her.

Stephanie clicked her nails against the water glass. She hadn't counted on this development. She was torn between wanting to meet them and fear of meeting them.

"It's up to you," Owen said, obviously reading her hesitation. "There is no obligation."

"This is a little surprising." She gave a short

laugh that sounded more strangled than mirthful. "Aren't they spread across the continent, if not the world?" she asked. "Do all of them want to meet me or only the ones here in Texas?"

"The entire clan. We've recently begun having family meetings by video-conference. This time they want to come to town."

Stephanie let out a long breath. All of them in one place at the same time. And all of their eyes trained on her, waiting for her to make a mistake.

"I know it sounds overwhelming, but they're a good bunch. We thought a small dinner at the house. You can bring a friend if it will make you feel more comfortable."

"You mean a date?"

"If you like." Stephanie saw him swallow. Then he picked up the glass of water and took a small drink. "Someone to give you support if you think we're a bit much."

"The last time I met members of your family one in particular didn't take to me. The other two were really into each other."

Owen looked a bit uncomfortable. "Digger and Erin consider themselves newlyweds. I've spoken to Rosa and she promises to be on her best behavior."

"When is this . . . dinner . . . to take place?" She felt it was more like an inquisition.

"Because of Rosa's modeling schedule, Dean's film, and Brad's hospital duties we can all get together next Saturday."

"In five days?"

He nodded.

The entire world was created in six days, Stephanie thought. If modeling, film and hospital schedules could be adjusted in five days, she ought to be ready to meet the Claytons in that amount of time. "All right."

"I'll let everyone know."

The waiter brought the check and Stephanie took it. Owen lifted it from her hand. "I'll charge it to the project."

She didn't argue, but collected her purse and papers and prepared to leave. Owen walked with her as they left the restaurant. He placed a guiding hand on her back at the door that led out into the July heat. The heat didn't even come close in comparison to the furnace that generated inside her.

Edging away from his hand, Stephanie walked toward the SUV bearing the logo for her design firm. She hadn't expected Owen to go with her, but he did. She pressed the electronic key to automatically unlock the doors. Owen opened the driver's door for her and she climbed into the seat. Before closing the door, he asked, "Will you be bringing a date?"

Stephanie took a moment to search his eyes. They were dark, unfathomable, and guarded, but intense and interested. She could feel a tenseness about him, however. He wanted to know. He wanted something from her, too, and she knew it. She wanted to reach up and encircle his neck, pull his mouth to hers and spend the afternoon exchanging slow, drugging kisses. She wanted him to make love to her. She wanted to know what all the women before her had learned. But she didn't want to be just one of them.

"I only ask so I know how many places to set at the table. We might need to add another leaf."

Stephanie slipped the key in the ignition and fired the engine. She returned her gaze to Owen.

"Add the leaf," she said.

Chapter Seven

Saturday night arrived all too soon. Stephanie had had her nails done, her hair styled, and she'd bought a new dress. Yet she felt anxious, ill at ease, disquieted, and wired. She vacillated between being overdressed and underdressed. What did one wear to meet a family? What did she call this grouping of people? They weren't related to her and they weren't related to each other. No bloodlines converged between any of them. Only Brad and Owen shared parents. The others were a collection of adopted children that had grown into adulthood together.

They had their shared past to bind them. Stephanie was the loner, the outsider. She'd insinuated herself into their lives and tonight was either her show or her showdown; she wasn't sure which.

"Stop obsessing, Hunter. This is what you wanted." Emilie spoke from the bedroom doorway. She was Stephanie's *date* tonight. If Stephanie needed moral support she trusted no one as much as she did Emilie. She knew Owen thought she was bringing a man.

He deserved it—probably thought it would be like a woman to taunt him with another man after they'd share searing kisses. Stephanie had played the game, but he'd hold the winning hand when Emilie arrived with her and not a man.

"I'm scared," Stephanie said.

"Why? You've already met half of them."

"That was casual and unexpected. Tonight is planned. And they'll all be there. All looking, staring, waiting for me to use the wrong fork or drink from my finger bowl."

"So don't do those things. They've already been done."

Stephanie choked on a laugh, then it broke through fully. Emilie joined her. The release was good. She could count on Emilie to help her out of any situation, although tonight would test her mettle.

"Let's go. You can't put off seeing him any longer."

"Him?"

"Yes, *him*. Don't look so surprised. You might say it's the other Claytons that are making you nervous, but I know only one of them makes your heart race and that's the big man himself—Owen."

"He does not."

"Hunter?"

After a moment of staring at each other, the two women left. "I'll drive," Emilie announced as she headed for her car. "In case, *he* wants to drive you home, you'll have no reason to refuse."

Stephanie gasped. "Emilie, we have an agreement. I work for him. And you are not to leave me alone with them."

Emilie dropped her purse in the car and got in.

"Just a technicality. How many women working for a man have ended up married to him?"

"Married? How did we get to marriage?"

"Well, this has got to be leading somewhere."

"You know, Forester" —Stephanie deliberately used Emilie's last name, letting her know she was serious—"I'm sorry I didn't ask Josh to come with me."

"She's here."

Stephanie heard the pronouncement before she rang the bell. Inside she could hear shuffling feet as if people were quickly trying to restore a room to its expected order or arrange themselves in casual positions so as not to appear anxious. She took a deep breath. The door opened and Dean stood there.

"Welcome," he said. "Please come in." His face bore a bright smile.

Stephanie's stomach clenched into a hard ball. She stepped inside with Emilie next to her. Quickly she introduced Emilie.

"We've been waiting for you," Dean said, closing the door and leading them toward the living room. Owen reached the bottom of the main stairway just as Stephanie and Emilie were about to pass it. Stephanie looked at Owen. He smiled and her face muscles relaxed as she returned it. While she'd dreaded seeing him with all his family, she was now glad he was there. The only real member of the Clayton clan whom she'd had more than a casual conversation with, he was her anchor and hopefully her needed support.

Despite Stephanie knowing about the meeting, her heart drummed in her ears. She was so close to getting what she'd vowed she wanted, yet so afraid the dream would end in ashes. She'd wanted a family all her life. She wanted to belong somewhere, know that no matter what, she could go to this place, this one place, and they would take her in and love her because that was what families did.

Yet she was here as a fraud. She didn't belong here. She hadn't grown up with this family, gone through the crises of life or the moments of happiness with them. She hadn't been here for the days of their lives when someone needed a shoulder to cry on, good news to share, or a party to throw. Although she had blood in her veins that matched the Claytons, she did not have the familial connection, the bonds that form families, tied them together and bring them to gatherings like the one before her.

"Hello, Clayton." Stephanie heard Emilie speaking. "I'm with Hunter tonight. Her moral support."

Owen looked surprised and relieved.

"We were at the Women's Museum together."

Owen looked from Emilie to Stephanie then back. "I remember. Good to see you again."

"Well, shall we go in?" Dean said.

Owen took Stephanie's hand. It was cold. "Don't worry," he whispered so only she could hear. "I'm the only wolf here tonight and you already know me."

Pulling her arm though his he escorted her into the next room. Dean and Emilie accompanied them a step back. The room was quiet when she entered it. The entire group was present and accounted for and all eyes were on her. Stephanie felt sweat on her back and hoped the tremor passing through her wasn't communicating itself to the man holding her arm.

"Everyone, this is Cynthia Clayton." Owen introduced her.

It felt strange to be called that. She had never been Cynthia Clayton that she could remember.

"Although I don't think she'll answer to that name," he continued. Again Stephanie had the feeling he could read her mind.

"Stephanie Hunter," she said. Her voice felt small in the room with so many people. She was nervous, but she wanted them to like her, to accept her. She couldn't remember ever having a test before that she so wanted to pass as this one. Calling on the skills she used every day and from years of practice meeting the public, she pulled her arm free and turned to Emilie. "This is my best friend, Emilie Forester."

"Hello," Emilie said. "I'm sure I'll learn your names as the night goes on."

The group nodded toward her. Then Stephanie walked over to Rosa and extended her hand. "It's so nice to see you again. I hope your trip to Sweden went well."

"It did." Rosa took her hand with a look of surprise. Stephanie had tried to find out as much as she could about them in the few days she had to prepare for this meeting. From Rosa's agency she had found out the young model was on assignment in Sweden. From Rosa Stephanie moved to Brad and his wife.

"Brad and Mallory." She shook hands with them. "We almost met at your wedding reception."

"Hello," Mallory spoke.

"I've read a couple of your articles on childhood development of adopted children."

The two doctors looked at each other. "Do you often read medical journals?" Brad asked.

"Only when there's an interesting subject. Or someone I'm going to meet the author in three days."

They laughed. Stephanie felt herself relaxing.

"Owen tells us you're a decorator," Brad said.

"I am. I went out on my own; I started eighteen months ago. And Owen's awarded me a very big job recently."

"One that she deserves," he added. "Hers was clearly the best bid. And it was a committee of three who chose the winner."

"We've heard you'll also be doing a television show on decorating." Digger or James Clayton's wife Erin said. "Hi, I'm Erin. We met at the museum."

It was Stephanie's turn to be surprised. She didn't think anyone knew about the show, despite the huge banner flying atop the Mercury Cable building. Stephanie moved to the two of them.

"It begins with the next season."

"Digger," He introduced himself. "We also met at the Women's Museum."

"I remember. You're in construction and Erin runs a day care facility."

They nodded, both with appreciative smiles that she knew what they did.

"Where is Sam? Is she with you?"

"She's spending the night with a friend she rarely gets to see since we live in Cobblersville."

"I'd like to meet her one day."

"We'll make a point of it," Erin said with a welcoming lift to her voice.

Luanne and Mark Rogers were last. Stephanie had only seen them once, at Brad and Mallory's wedding. She had circled the room and all eyes were on her. With the smiles she'd received from each family member, she felt as if the tense air that had been in the room when she entered it now had slices cut in it that allowed a flowing breeze to pass through.

"Hello," Stephanie said to Luanne. "If I'm right, you're Luanne. You work for child welfare in Cobblersville and Mark is a geologist."

"You've done your homework," Mark said. He extended his hand with a warm smile and a twinkle in his eye that told her she was doing all right. Silently Stephanie thanked him for his encouragement.

"Now we want to know something about you," Dean stated.

"Why don't we go in and eat first?" Owen was by her side and she hadn't seen him move. Stephanie was so relieved, without knowing what she was doing, she reached behind her and grabbed his hand. "I'm sure Stephanie will be more willing to tell us all about herself after the meal."

They moved to the dining room where Stephanie was sure the interrogation would occur. She suspected Rosa was holding her barbs, but would deliver them before the dinner was over. So far she'd been very congenial. Maybe Owen had told her there was nothing between them so there was no reason for her to feel as if her brother would be taken away from her. Stephanie wasn't sure if the younger woman had seen her grab Owen's hand. Or witnessed him squeezing it in return.

If Stephanie had planned this event she would have had it catered with white-gloved waiters providing a gourmet meal, complete with chilled icing-designed plates holding a carefully choreographed concoction for dessert. But the Claytons were a family and the meal was served by all the members. Bowls were passed around the table and each person served themselves. The smells about the

room had her stomach telling her that it was good
food.

Dean had cooked steaks that were thick, tender,
and juicy. Foil-covered baked potatoes were stacked
on a plate like a silver Christmas tree. A variety of
vegetables shared space, creating a colorful palate
against the white table cloth. Stephanie stole a
glance at Owen. How could he have known that
this was exactly the way she wanted a family to be?

The men were active with lots of talk and jokes.
Laughter seemed to be the word for the day.
Finally, as the meal came to an end, they got
around to her.

"So, Stephanie, tell us about yourself," Dean repeated the same question he'd asked in the other
room.

Stephanie had relaxed, but with the question,
her antennae went up and she realized she was
center stage.

"Owen tells us you only discovered you were
Cynthia Clayton recently," Brad added.

She didn't know what to make of Brad. His
question was serious and he had a stern look, but
she'd seen him smile and his face was totally different when he did.

"Why don't you tell me what you know, so I can
fill in the parts I know." She specifically said it that
way because she didn't know her entire history, either.

Brad shrugged. "Fair," he said, folding his hand
on the table. "According to the report from the investigator . . ."

She lost what he was saying. Investigator? She
looked at Owen. His face was unreadable, but she
knew it was *him.* He'd had her investigated and not
told her.

" . . . came back to Dallas then and lived with

your aunt and uncle." Brad was laying her life out for her. It sounded strange to have it related so concisely, as if she were a prisoner about to be sentenced. Yet all he'd told her was the newspaper account. There was nothing more to his report.

A hush fell over the room when his voice faded. All eyes turned to her. It was time to tell her story.

"I didn't know anything until I was sixteen. My mother and father loved me. I didn't know they weren't my real parents or even that my father didn't know my mother had stolen me. They did everything parents should do for their children. Holidays, vacations, dance lessons, baseball games. They encouraged us in everything we wanted to try. Then when I was twelve they died in a car accident."

She watched the faces around her. Emilie smiled, giving her courage. Owen winked at her over the coffee cup he lifted to his mouth.

"When I found out I was adopted . . ." She related the story of how she'd discovered her birth parents. "It was only a few days before your wedding" —she looked at Brad and Mallory— "that I found out my real name and real parents. I knew I should have stayed away, but I wanted to meet them. I wanted to know who they were." She looked down at her half-eaten plate of food. "Then Devon had her heart attack and died."

"They never told you?" Rosa asked.

Stephanie shook her head. Rosa's face was as beautiful as any fashion model's could be. This time, however, Stephanie saw compassion in her eyes.

"They don't know that I know now," she confessed. "I have three brothers. Only one of them knows."

"Why didn't you tell them?" Rosa asked again.

Even with incredulity in her voice, there was also wonder.

Stephanie wanted to get up. She felt confined behind the table with everyone looking at her.

"My aunt never really took to me. We don't have a lot in common." Including bloodlines, she thought. "My uncle has been ill and I didn't want to add anymore stress to his life. Emilie knows everything I know."

Emilie smiled. She'd been quiet most of the night.

"Why didn't you come to us and tell us?" Luanne asked.

"You all grew up together. You are a family and while I was Devon and Reuben's child, we" —she circled the room with her hand— "have no connection. After she died I thought it was better to not interfere."

"But you did." Dean spoke again. "You were at the wedding and the funeral."

"I can't explain that, not so you'd understand." Stephanie took a breath. She wanted them to know how she felt, but she didn't want to say things that would make them dislike her.

"Try us," Digger challenged. "We really want to know."

Stephanie watched the other heads nod and wished she hadn't said anything. As much as Digger softened his "try us" comment, he and everyone else wanted to know her reason.

Taking a deep breath, she plunged ahead. "I thought it would be different." Stephanie kept her head up. She wanted to drop it and look down at her hands like a child caught doing something wrong, but she refused to do so. "I wanted so much to feel something. I wanted grief, unhappiness, a sense of loss, something. I thought that when I found my birth mother I would know her. I would be able to cut through the years of lost time and connect with her." She paused. "It didn't happen. I felt nothing. I was sorry she died, as sorry as I could feel for the death of any person, but it wasn't the grief I felt when my . . ." She was about to say when her real mother died, but she stopped herself and finished with, " . . . when I was twelve. I thought I should go to the funeral. She *was* my mother, even if she didn't know me and I didn't know her. It was the least I could do out of respect for the life she led." Carefully she looked at the expectant faces. Some of them had dropped their heads, undoubtedly remembering Devon Clayton and what she had meant to their lives. "I know she was your mother. You lived with her for years. You knew her, grew to love her. You can remember her smile, a happy glint in her eyes, a surprised expression. To me she was a stranger."

"We'll tell you about her," Rosa said. "I was the youngest among the adopted Claytons. Owen is the oldest. He's got the longest memory."

"Digger came first," Owen corrected her. "He was already here when Brad and I came."

"We have long memories, Stephanie," Digger told her. "We'll tell you so many stories, you'll feel like you were here when they happened."

Stephanie blinked away a sudden mist that threatened her eyes. She smiled at the family. Had they accepted her? She was unsure. Rosa hadn't wanted her around at their first meeting. And she didn't know who she was then. Was she only putting on a front now? Stephanie had known too many times when she thought she was being accepted only to find out later that it wasn't so. Her aunt had taught her well. Was *this* family repeating that same procedure?

Her gaze went to Owen. She wanted to trust him, wanted to believe that honor and dignity meant something to them all, but they had had her investigated. Owen had asked for and been given a DNA sample. They knew practically everything about her life and all she knew about them were their occupations and that they were a close-knit family who protected their own.

And that she could lose herself in Owen Clayton's arms.

Emilie refused dessert and pleaded an early morning appointment as a reason to leave.

"I have an appointment, too," Stephanie said. "Sorry to eat and run, but my ride appears to be leaving."

She stood up.

"There's no need to leave," Dean jumped in. "There are a hundred cars here. We'd like you to stay. One of us can drive you home later."

Stephanie nodded and threw Emilie a look that said she would get even with her.

While the table was cleared and coffee served in the living room, Dean put on some music and couples paired off in the various chairs. Stephanie found herself sitting next to Owen on a love seat. She could feel the heat of his body and her heart beat wildly.

This has got to stop, she told herself. The two had agreed to only work together on a professional footing. These feelings had no place in her life.

Dean began one of the stories involving his father and himself. It had something to do with his camera and a set of photos that had no place in a sixteen-year-old's room. Everyone laughed remembering the incident. Stephanie sat outside of the shared history, feeling more alone in the crowd than if she'd been home curled up on her sofa.

Stories went on for an hour before Owen stated they had tired her out and she needed to get home. He agreed to drive her, fulfilling the promise to Emilie, and Emilie's manipulation of Stephanie's nonexistent love life.

As soon as the car door closed and Owen reversed out of the driveway, Stephanie asked, "Why didn't you tell me you'd had me investigated?"

Her anger had been present ever since she heard the comment delivered as if it was a known fact. She'd been holding in the rage that had gone through her. After smiling, kissing cheeks, shaking hands and saying good night, she exploded on Owen.

"It wasn't like that." He tried to pacify her. "We hired a private investigator to find you."

"That's all. Just to find out where I was?"

His hesitation told her there was more. "Where you were and if you were really their daughter."

"What else?"

"That's all."

"So you have a report that shows you my address and possibly my birth certificate?"

"Not exactly."

"I want to see it."

"I don't have to show it to you."

"And I didn't have to lick your cotton swab or have a needle stuck into my arm." She thrust her arm out as if he could see the puncture where they'd drawn her blood. "If you know something about me, I want to know what it is."

"You don't trust us." Owen stopped at a red light. He stared at her. Stephanie kept her eyes on the road ahead.

"Why should I trust you? Any of you? You look and act as if I have done something wrong. As if I'm some sinister lost relative who suddenly appears to cheat you out of the family fortune."

"The family has no fortune."

"And I didn't invite myself into it."

"I know that." He started the car again and drove straight to the condominium building where she lived.

Stephanie was out of the car the moment it stopped. Owen was only a second behind her. "Stop," he called, but she kept walking. Jogging quickly he caught up with her and stepped in front to stop her pace. Holding her upper arms with both his hands, he asked, "Why are you so angry?"

"I don't like people prying into my life. How would you feel if someone unknown to you had you investigated? Then they could lay your life out in front of you like the carcass of a castrated bull."

Owen dropped his arms. "I never thought of it like that. I was following my mother's request. When we found her papers telling about your kidnapping, we thought it best to find you. There was no other ulterior motive."

"Why didn't *you* tell me? Why did you leave me to learn about it in a roomful of strangers who dropped the little nuclear device as if it were no more important than yesterday's weather?"

"I apologize. I'm sorry. What more can I say?"

"I want to see it," she stated. Her voice was strong and unopen to argument.

"There isn't much of importance in it."

"Credit rating?"

He didn't deny it.

"Business relationships, debts owed by my business, personal investments, former jobs?"

He nodded, letting her know it was all there.

"Past boyfriends?"

After a moment of hesitation he nodded confirmation.

Stephanie held her breath for a long moment. She was ready to explode, but kept her emotions in check. When she was able to speak, her voice was soft and controlled.

"With all the women in your own life, why would you need to voyeur into mine? What could you possibly be looking for?" She started to walk away then turned back. "I want that complete report delivered to me tomorrow. Leave nothing out of it."

She pulled the glass door open and walked into the building, keeping her back straight and her head up. She could feel Owen's eyes boring into her. She waited for an elevator and stepped inside. As the doors reduced his image to a slit, then obliterated it completely, she crumpled against the wall.

"He knows," she said aloud. "He knows everything."

The night air blew through the open windows as Owen drove back toward his house and waiting family. He thought about how angry Stephanie had been when she heard Brad's slip about the investigator. Owen had intended to tell her. He was going to the day he drove to her office, let her know that was how they had found her, but she eclipsed his message by telling him she already knew her parentage, then driving away. After that it slipped his mind. He never got to it again.

Brad assumed she knew. Owen had told the family the contents of the original report. He had kept to himself the message of the second one. Finding Cynthia Clayton had been easy. Technically the job ended there, but Owen wanted to know more. He'd asked Simon Thalberg to find out about Stephanie Hunter. Initially he thought, told himself, he was doing it for the family. That they needed to know what kind of person Stephanie Hunter was, but the truth was she was getting under his skin and *he* wanted to know what kind of person she was.

What he found out he kept to himself, although most of it proved she was the kind of person his parents would be proud to call their own. Her credit rating was good now, but it hadn't always been that way. She had three younger brothers and had been raised by an eighth grade schoolteacher aunt named Meriweather Carter and her uncle a general practitioner named Jackson Carter. She'd excelled in school and participated in sports. Her aunt made her life a living hell and during her early teens she ran away constantly, living on the streets and stealing to eat. Her story reminded him of Digger's and his heart softened toward and her plight.

Her uncle got her in counseling with the promise that she could go away to college. She graduated high school and immediately began a summer program before her freshman year. Withdrawn and lonely she met Darren Parker at a college mixer. She was ripe for him. Darren was the local campus pusher and Stephanie was to be his next victim.

On their way to a party early in their relationship, Darren stopped for beer and robbed the liquor store. During the ensuing chase, Darren lost control of the car and the two went over an embankment. He was killed and Stephanie was critically wounded. When she woke and was able to understand what had happen, she was not only charged with being an accomplice to a robbery, but discovered she had been pregnant. She miscarried as a result of the accident. Spending a month in the hospital, she was then released into her uncle's custody. After hearing her story and that of other students with firsthand accounts of Darren's exploits, the judge let her off.

From then on she became a model student, keeping to herself and avoiding other students as much as possible. Until she met Emilie. And her life changed. She found out there were other people in the world like her.

Adopted.

"This is all my fault." Stephanie paced in the narrow space between the chairs in the hospital's nurses lounge. She and Emilie were alone in the room. Emilie started work in half an hour. She lay easily in an overstuffed chair while Stephanie blew off steam. "I should have left the past alone. No one ever finds anything good when they start poking into people's lives."

"Don't be so hard on yourself, Hunter. It's not the end of the world."

"No." She glared at her friend. "It could be the end of my business. I've barely got it in the black and this happens."

"You don't know that Owen has the information. And if he does, there's no indication that he will use it for illicit purposes."

"He can hold it over my head, stifle my business or wait until I really get on good footing and use it against me."

Emily sat up in the chair. "Do you really think he's that kind of man?"

Stephanie stopped pacing and dropped down next to Emilie. "Of course, not," she said, feeling defeated. "Darren Parker existed a lifetime ago. Yet he's going to follow me the rest of my life."

"You know people are more tolerant these days than they used to be. And the court dropped your case."

"I'm working for the elite in this town. Character means everything to them."

"Hunter, the charges were dropped. There is nothing for anyone to find that means anything."

"What about the baby?"

"You're not the first person to get pregnant. And you lost the baby before you knew there was one. Do you think Rusty Shulman wouldn't have hired you if you have a child? Or that Olivia wouldn't recommend you if you had a child at home and no husband? Be real, Hunter. This is a new millennium."

Emilie stood up and moved to a chair directly in front of Stephanie. She leaned back, crossing her ankles and looked Stephanie directly in the eye. "The truth is," she said quietly, "you wonder what Owen Clayton thinks of you now that he knows."

For a long moment the two friends stared at each other. Finally Stephanie dropped her eyes and leaned back in the chair.

"I do," she admitted.

"So what is your problem? He can't judge you for something you did in your youth. Lord knows he's had an active life and look how far up the ladder he's climbed and continues to climb."

"He is man. And that makes a difference."

"As does his reputation?"

"That, too," Stephanie admitted. "Why should he be interested in me for anything more than a short-term bed partner? Something I am not interested in being. And the rest of his family didn't like me, either." She changed the subject from Owen.

"I thought they were very nice to you."

"They were. Too nice. The kind of nice when they really don't like you. I had the feeling they thought I was there to steal the family silver."

"You're reading too much into it. They seemed like really nice people. And the fact that they were all adopted into the same family and they are so closely aligned to each other is impressive. They have to understand your predicament."

"I see. They impressed you."

Emilie spread her hands in a defeated gesture. "They impressed me. I wish my own family was as close as they seem to be."

Stephanie wished that too. She knew Emilie's family was exactly like the Claytons. They poured love on her to the point it was visible. But Stephanie had long ago given up on her aunt ever coming around to liking her. She wouldn't go so far as to ask for her love. Not anymore. She'd wanted it, prayed that one day she would wake up and find that Aunt Meriweather had come to love her; but it never happened and unless she wanted something from Stephanie, which she'd die before asking for it, the two would live as related enemies.

"Well, what are you going to do?"

"Do?"

"You've always taken action before. When you have a problem, it's act, do something, solve it." Emilie smacked the back of one hand into her palm, punctuating each phrase.

"Not this time. I suppose they will all fly back to wherever they came from and I'll go on with my decorating." She hunched her shoulders. "They've met me now. What more is there?"

"What more do you want?"

* * *

Emilie's question was still plaguing Stephanie as she negotiated the traffic back to West Holiday. What more did she want? Did she want to be part of the Clayton family or part of Owen's family? Or were they one and the same? Did she want anything more to do with them at all?

She called Marian Morton from her car and found everything at the shop was under control. Her young assistant was both enthusiastic and efficient. Then, deciding to take some action, Stephanie turned the SUV toward the *Dallas Herald* building site.

She supposed the pivotal link in the decision rested with her association with Owen Clayton. He pushed all her buttons and some of them he didn't even know he pushed. She denied it to Emilie and to herself, but Owen was the reason she'd wanted so badly for his family to accept her. Yet the only one she thought did was Dean. He happily wore his feelings right out front. Erin and Mallory, married Claytons, also liked her. Luanne was unreadable. Rosa, on the other hand, cleverly concealed her feelings the night of the dinner. Brad was straight-faced and hard to read and Digger appeared genuine.

Stephanie still felt she had no place with them. The tie that would have bound them, Devon and Reuben Clayton, was broken. They were all adults, grown people, without the need for a lost sister or a family friend. She was independent, embarking on her own career. She didn't need them with their varied personalities. Breaking through to them or understanding them would garner her nothing. But it could hurt her if she let her emotions embrace them and found rejection on their part.

The *Dallas Herald* was nowhere near complete,

but walls were going up and the inner structure was being closed in. Stephanie pulled past the construction vehicles and parked the SUV in a safe place. While she'd made some preliminary sketches and samples, she needed exact measurements now. She would need to place special orders and line up crews before her meeting with the three men who would occupy the spaces. She wanted to have a clear idea of the dimensions so she could present a well-balanced plan.

Not letting Owen know she was coming proved a mistake. The moment the elevator cage doors opened and she stepped into the all white corridor she could see him among the workmen in the distance. He turned at the exact moment and their eyes locked. Stephanie's stomach lurched and the box holding her electronic measuring tools, pencil and papers seemed to weigh her arm down. She wanted to back into the elevator and return to the first level, but she couldn't. She needed to see him, confront the aftermath of the night before and find ground on which she would walk for her future.

Owen stopped what he was doing and walked toward her. While the other workmen wore T-shirts and carpenter's pants, Owen had on a brown short-sleeved shirt, khaki's, and a hard hat. He picked up another hat on his way toward her. Stephanie wanted him to smile at her, give her some indication that last night wasn't the total disaster she had made of it, but he didn't.

"Hello," he said. "I wasn't expecting you." He handed her the hat. She placed it on her head, knowing this was a construction area and safety rules required she wear it.

She knew they had an agreement about her presence here, not that they had adhered to it from the moment they agreed to the terms, but it still existed.

"I came on the moment," she said. "But I'm glad you're here. I think we need to talk. I was a little irrational last night."

Behind them someone dropped something and the crash echoed through the empty floor. Owen turned. A man waved, indicating everyone was all right. A can of joint compound lay on its side.

"Why don't we step over here?" He spread a hand to lead them to a huge walled-in area with galactic-size windows. At this level the windows had been installed. The room was exceedingly hot. Outside the city stood in all its glass and steel glory. Stephanie walked to the windows and panned the view. The day was clear and she could see forever.

Owen stood at her side. "You know once my brother made a complete replica of downtown out of Lego."

"Which brother?"

"Digger. He does construction in Cobblersville."

"I remember. He's married to Erin, the nursery school owner."

"You're beginning to know us."

"Owen?" She turned to him. "I don't know how to say this. Last night—well, it didn't turn out like I expected. I mean, I wanted to meet all of you, but I was so surprised to find out—" She stopped.

"I know. Brad wouldn't have said that if he didn't think you already knew. We weren't prying. It was how we found our birth mother. We thought it was the natural thing to do in trying to find you. But I didn't leave it there."

"What did you do?"

He swallowed. "The family only authorized an investigator to find you. When he located Cynthia Clayton, I went a step further and asked him to check you out, who you were and what you might want from us. The rest of the family doesn't know I did that and I didn't share any of the information with them."

"So, only you know about . . ."

He nodded before she finished the sentence.

"Why did you do it?"

"Family," he answered simply. "You don't understand the closeness we developed. We're a very protective lot. We had to be since most of us remember being shuffled from family to family. We built up defenses to protect ourselves, our emotions. When we found the Claytons—or they found us—a bond was formed that we hadn't known before. It makes us a family, and families protect each other."

"You needed protection from me?"

"In a manner of speaking. You appeared in our lives at a point when stress factors were at a high point and emotions were close to the surface. You didn't tell us who you were, even though you knew. It only made me more suspicious that you really wanted something from us when you told me you already knew Devon and Reuben were your parents."

"What could I have wanted?"

"Money, a share of their estate, some kind of vindication, family scandal, notoriety in the press. This could draw attention to your business and possibly draw in clients. Everyone loves a scandal, especially one that mars the reputation of two good people. Our parents were model citizens. Not only in our eyes, but in everyone's eyes."

Stephanie opened her mouth in surprise. "And you think—"

"It's been done before," he interrupted her.

"I would never do that."

"I know that now, but I didn't at the time."

She walked away from him, needing space.

"Stephanie, I didn't find anything that you need to be ashamed of. We all make bad decisions when we're young."

She smiled, but her eyes were closer to tears than mirth. "Emilie said the same thing, but as you know, in this business image is everything. I'm dealing with clients at the top of society. They believe that my reputation is as clean as the paint on their walls."

"And it is."

"What happened to the report?"

"You said you wanted it."

She nodded.

"I had it sent to your home. It's the only copy."

Except for the one that was burned into his memory.

"Thank you," she said, feeling slightly grateful. She couldn't remove what he'd already read. "Now, I'd better get to work."

"Wait a minute."

She stopped in mid-stride.

"What about the other part of last night? The family?"

"They've met me. What else is there?"

He walked to where she stood. "What else? Don't you want to get to know them? Let them know you?"

"What would be the point? You are a family. I am not a part of it."

She turned and left him. She didn't want to be part of the Claytons anymore. She didn't want to join their family meetings and discuss things as if she had always been with them. She didn't want to see Owen across a room or on a television screen and remember the tender way he'd held her in his arms.

She wanted him totally and completely, but he wasn't ready for that kind of commitment. Stephanie wasn't sure if he would ever be. But she was sure she wouldn't hang her heart out on his bedpost and let him use it on a temporary basis.

They had an agreement and from now on she would stick to it.

Chapter Eight

Life was a set of routines. Owen was indulging in one of his, driving fast through the streets of Dallas. He should be on his way to Jake's for a leisurely meal or a client meeting. He had lived by routines all his life. From shaving and showering in the morning to checking, rechecking, cross-checking, and double-checking every aspect of his plans before allowing a single shovel of land to be turned; to watching old horror flicks on the TV in his stocking feet and eating double-buttered popcorn. There had been interruptions to his routines, but after a reasonable time lapse he'd settled back into methods that were tried and true. Since meeting Stephanie Hunter he felt as if his life had been altered. Thoughts of her, seeing her, wanting to see her, had consumed him far more than anyone else in his past.

Her rejection of him and his family had come as a surprise. Owen wasn't used to women walking away from him. Since he was sixteen he'd been able to get any woman he wanted. He discovered he could charm them and he'd perfected that charm, worked it to his advantage until women were like a game to him. His friends had known better than to bet against his timing in getting a date with the woman of his choice since he was in high school. With each new woman he'd shave a few seconds off the conquest.

He was acutely aware of the tactic of hard-to-get, but he always prevailed, outwitting even the strongest objections to attain what he wanted. Then Stephanie Hunter dropped into his life. And she was the enigma. She said she wasn't interested in him and she meant it. With her it wasn't a game. She was serious.

Her rejection of his family should have been the seal on his feelings for anything having to do with her emotionally, but it only seemed to make her more desirable. He hadn't seen her in a week, not since that day at the *Dallas Herald* offices after the family dinner.

The family liked her, even Rosa had changed her mind about Stephanie. She'd conquered Dean with her smile. But Dean thought Owen's lifestyle was emotionally challenged if not destructive and he'd chosen Stephanie as the cure for it. She could, he admitted. Owen no longer thought Stephanie knew anything about the bank account with her name on it, but in the back of his mind was still that niggling mistrust of women. She'd come into their lives too conveniently and while everything he'd found out about her rang true, something still bothered him. She could just be a good actress—a damn good actress—and a superb manipulator. Yet all his brain cells were trying to convince him that she was something else. It was that something else that was emotionally scaring him. Maybe he should take her advice and let things go. They could work together and when the job ended they would each go their own way.

He'd sent her the file that Simon Thalberg had given him, and he thought little of what had happened to her during her college years was her fault. She was lucky to get out of it with no consequences. At least none you could see. He knew from talking to his sister-in-law Erin that losing a baby could be emotionally draining and something parents accepted, but never forgot. Owen never intended to marry or have children, although he had some experience with what they went through. He'd watched his brother Digger go through hell when his son from his first marriage died in an accident.

Then he thought of his niece, Samantha. She was a happy little girl and he loved her dearly. If anything happened to her it would kill his brother and he was unsure what it would do to his heart.

Instead of pulling into the parking lot at Jake's, Owen whipped the car around the corner and drove downtown and into the customer parking lot at Mercury Cable. Getting out he closed the door and pocketed the keys, then leaned against the hood to wait for Stephanie. He'd called her office and been told by her new assistant that Stephanie was at the studio filming for her show.

Owen had seen commercials on television announcing the coming of her design show. The cable station was making a big splash for the program. He smiled at her celebrity. He knew his parents would be proud of her, their only child, making good. Above him was a large banner with her smiling face and the show's name written in different colors.

Owen was still looking at it when she came out

of the building and headed toward her SUV in the employee parking lot.

"Stephanie," he called, jogging across the asphalt. She turned, surprise evident on her face. Owen was afraid to read it. He knew they had an agreement, but this wasn't work. This was family. And he *had* to see her, regardless of her wishes to avoid seeing him.

"Owen, what are you doing here?"

"Marian told me you were here and I wanted to talk to you." She looked uncomfortable and stepped away from him. He wondered what that meant. "Do you mind if we go somewhere?"

"I'm afraid I'm on my way to an appointment. Does this have anything to do with the *Dallas Herald?*"

"It's about the family." He saw her visibly stiffen. "What about joining me for dinner?" The idea came to him in a flash and unlike his usual routine of deciding what he wanted to do before he'd done it, the question was out without a second thought.

"You mean like a *date?*"

"I can call it a business meeting if you'd like though it's not business I want to discuss. It's family. I want to talk to you about dinner with them."

"Oh," she said.

She thought a moment. Sweat was collecting on Owen's brow. He could say the heat and humidity was the cause, but he knew it was Stephanie; her closeness, the smell of her hair and the way she'd gotten under his skin was making him nervous and causing his body to yearn for hers. He wanted her to say she would go so badly he was willing her to respond positively.

"My appointment won't be over until late. I couldn't be ready before eight o'clock."

"Fine." He smiled. "I'll pick you up then." He

said good-bye and turned to leave. He had a date. Owen hadn't been so giddy since he was thirteen and the prettiest girl in school agreed to go to the movies with him. He wanted to look back at Stephanie but didn't. He didn't want her to know that his feet were hardly touching the ground.

Stephanie's bedroom didn't look anything like it had on the night she was having dinner with the Claytons. Tonight it was neat and clean. She'd pulled out one outfit and the decision was made. The red chiffon. Everything about her from the skin out was red. Her strapless bra and underwear sported the same color as her polished blood red fingernails. With her skin color the effect would be dramatic.

She didn't know what Owen would say about dinner with his family. She was ready to hold her temper, but if the need arose she was ready for anything he had to discuss with her.

Her appointment had been with the bank. They refused to renew her loan and wouldn't extend her current payments. She needed money quickly to infuse her business. Her commission for the *Dallas Herald* wouldn't come through until she finished the job and that was months away. She had to make trips, provide designs for approval, hire contractors. Her expenses were more than the advances she'd get prior to completion. Without a loan she wouldn't be financially able to complete the job. She should have stuck by her refusal of the job when she'd sent it to Owen. But then she'd seen him and in the full light of their face-to-face meeting and the intense aura of her feelings she did the only thing she could. She accepted the business.

She had to dazzle the *Herald's* owners. This was the largest job she'd ever done, bigger than anything she'd done while working for Josh, and she had to make it her absolute best. It was a make or break job and she knew it. The hungry eyes of the decorating world were trained on her, especially those firms who'd been passed over when the bid was awarded to her. An upstart. A one-plus-year out of the pasture firm. They were all waiting for her to fail. If she didn't get financing, she would fail and the failure would relegate her to a small-time business and that is where she would stay.

Stephanie finished her makeup and hair as a knock came on the door. She looked at the clock. Owen was on time. Taking one final look, she slipped her feet into her favorite shoes and headed toward a man she should be running from.

"Wow!" Owen said, taking a step back. "I see you're not dressed for Jake's."

The truth was she was appropriately dressed for Jake's. "Would you like me to change?" She had no intention of doing so. She felt confident in this dress. It was soft and flowing, but to her it was made of armor.

"Absolutely not." His voice was decisive, low with a quality that could have been a catcall.

"Shall we go, then?"

Owen offered his arm and Stephanie hesitated. She didn't want to touch him. She knew the feel of shock that skittered up her arm each time the two made contact. It was a feeling she welcomed and dreaded. It was a good feeling, pleasant, warm, inviting trust. She dreaded it because it *was* a good feeling, pleasant, warm, inviting trust—and she couldn't trust Owen. She wanted to. She truly wanted to put everything on the table, discuss what both of them felt regarding their strange situation. But she thought Owen was holding something back. There was something he knew or felt that he wasn't telling her. He was protective of his parents. She expected that, even admired it, but what was it about them that was such a secret? Or did the secret have to do with someone else?

He pulled into the parking lot of The Mart. Like many of the Dallas's downtown buildings, there was a restaurant on the top floor. The Mart was really the Merchandising Mart, a block-size, eight-story building showcasing furniture. Everything from early American to ultra modern could be found in the various displays. While Stephanie had spent many hours going through them and selecting furniture for her clients, she had never been to the top-floor restaurant. The walls and ceiling were dark blue. Tiny white lights studded the ceiling, effectively looking like stars in a faraway galaxy.

Owen had reserved a table near windows which curved downward to the floor and looked out over the city. It was set in an intimate area and when seated Stephanie had the feeling they were floating under the stars without a floor beneath them. It was strange and wonderful and exactly the way she often felt when Owen was around. The whole effect was impressive. She relaxed, forgetting the encounter she'd had with the loan manager at the bank and slipping into a more serene posture.

"You're perfect in this setting," Owen told her.

Charm oozed from him. Stephanie couldn't call him on it. As long as she knew he was charming her, it was all right. When the waiter brought the drinks they'd ordered, Owen raised his glass.

"To Stephanie Hunter," he toasted.

She smiled and nodded. They drank.

"I see commercials for your new TV show are airing frequently."

She was pleased they were on and also pleased he'd seen them. Stephanie didn't picture him as a man who watched television, but she knew he liked old movies.

"The station is making a grand push" —she used her hand to indicate quote marks—"for the program."

"Is it fun?"

"Ever so much. I'd never been to a television studio before this came about."

"How did that happen?"

Owen had leaned in and appeared genuinely interested in what she would be doing. But, she reminded herself, charming men always did. It was part of the act. He slipped into the role with such ease that she was unsure he even knew it was an act. Yet, she answered him.

"The idea came one night as I was flipping through some magazines looking for new ideas or inspiration to complete a project for a client. I saw a layout of a home in Chicago. Everything was perfect about it. It reminded me of a television set, a designed space that had perfect scale and intelligent lighting." She pause to take a drink of water. "Then I thought it would be nice to tell the average homemaker a few tips on how to make a room in their own home look as perfect as the one in the magazine."

"So you approached the studio?"

"I called Design TV with the idea. They weren't that enthusiastic about it. Apparently they get hundreds of ideas. Everyone wants to be on TV."

"So how did you get through the maze and have your proposal accepted?" Stephanie wondered if he was remembering how she got him to accept her proposal for the *Dallas Herald* job. The story was similar.

"After the idea crystalized in my mind, I really wanted the exposure. I felt it would help my company and bring in added finances." She held back on telling him how much more important the finances were than the exposure on the screen. "I designed a set in miniature—"

"Like you'd done for me?"

"Similarly. I outlined my programs and partnered with a local college to use some of the television students as camera men and film editors. I produced a pilot video of the first three programs and went back and made a presentation in which I would be the producer."

"And they accepted it?"

"Not right away. Almost a year later, after I'd given up on the idea, I got a call that they wanted the show and would I come in to discuss it. After several months of negotiations, production finally began. And then things happened at warp speed."

"You obviously enjoy it."

"It's a lot of work, but the crew makes it fun."

"Well I hope it runs for a long time." He took a sip of his drink.

"Thanks. So do I. I could use the money."

Their meals arrived. The food was expertly arranged on the plates for position, color, and proportion, nothing like the family-style meal she'd had with Owen's family.

"Money?" His eyes pierced into hers and she noticed how stiff his body became.

"It takes a lot of capital to get a business up and running."

"I thought everything was going well for you."

"It is. Since I finished Rusty Shulman's offices and getting the *Dallas Herald* contract was a definite coup, but there are still things that need financing. When I proposed the idea of the television show, it wasn't only for prestige and the possibility of future business. I wanted the added income to support the business."

"Do you always go after what you want with this much" —He stopped, searching for the right word— "stalwart passion?"

No one had ever characterized her this way before. *Stalwart passion.* Her? Stephanie put down her fork and knife and smiled. Not getting the bank loan no longer seemed like a problem. It floated away on an invisible air current and passed through the starry ceiling without any disturbance to the twinkling lights.

"I suppose I do."

He nodded. "I like that in a woman."

He did? Stephanie's eyes opened wide. She wouldn't have thought he took the time to access any other qualities about the women he dated except their measurements. Since she'd become so involved with him and his family, Stephanie devoured all the information she found on them. Well, on Owen at least. It wasn't hard. It seemed each time she looked for something in the decorating world his name came up.

He was well known in architectural circles. Emilie had given her some details on Owen's love of women, but Stephanie had continued her own research. Reading between the lines, she discovered his known reputation for the softer sex. Josh was forthcoming with anything she needed to know, but he also told her Owen was trustworthy and fair in all areas except romance.

"Don't get involved with him," Josh had warned. "Owen Clayton doesn't trust women and he'll break your heart if you give him the chance."

It was too late, Stephanie thought. Emilie had first seen it in her, but now Stephanie admitted it. Looking across the table at him her entire body prickled with electrical impulses. She was sure she could have lighted the ceiling using her own power.

"What about us?" he asked, snapping the thoughts in her head. She hadn't been listening to him.

"Us?"

"The family. Do you have as much passion for us?"

Stephanie was disappointed. She thought he was talking about them. The two of them. Not his sisters and brothers.

"That's not a fair question," she told him.

"Why?" He spread his hands, looking innocent.

"Well, when you're dealing in personal relationships, passion needs to flow in both directions. And the passion coming from your family is dislike for me."

"You're imagining that. They really like you."

"Maybe Erin and Mallory. They married Claytons. They don't have the same bonds that the others have. And they don't look at me as an interloper. I am. And I understand that. They have no reason to like or dislike me. The best thing I can do is stay away from you all."

"Is that why you made all those demands to work with me?"

She took a sip of her drink to buy herself time. It was part of the reason. She could easily agree with him and not have to explain anything further, but Stephanie wouldn't take the easy way out.

She was sitting across from Owen. She got up and moved around to the seat closest to him.

"Owen, I am attracted to you. I know your reputation—" She stopped him when he tried to interrupt her. "Don't deny it."

"I wasn't going to."

"I apologize." Stephanie realized how her comment had sounded. "I'm also building a business and it's consuming all my free time. If I'm going to support myself as an independent designer, then I have to give it my attention. I can't afford a complication in my life right now."

"I'm glad I'm a complication and I haven't completely lost my touch."

Stephanie smiled, knowing his comment was designed to lighten the mood. She put her hand on his and his fingers tightened around hers. "So you understand?"

He nodded. "However, the passion you speak of isn't only one way."

Stephanie looked into his eyes and undisguised need was apparent there. She felt herself melting. Owen leaned toward her, still holding her hand. Stephanie automatically leaned toward him. His mouth touched hers. She was glad they were semi-concealed from the rest of the diners, yet when Owen's free hand slipped under her hair and he fused his mouth to hers, she no longer cared if they were standing in the middle of Main Street at noon.

She didn't care if they were mixing business with pleasure. The pleasure ruled out every argument. Owen lifted his head and repositioned his mouth. His thumb drew gentle circles on the sensitive skin under her ear. Stephanie tried to remain in control, but her mind and body were at odds and her body won. Her hand slipped up his arm and she squeezed tight.

After a moment they separated. Stephanie had

no breath. She drew in a lung full of air and slowly let it out. Dropping her head, she hid her features from him so he couldn't see how affected she was by his kiss.

"I suppose," she began, "my comments about keeping this on a strictly business level just got shot to hell?"

What Stephanie ate for dinner would elude her forever. If they talked any more about his family, she had no memory of it. The kiss was the only thing she could pull into focus. The drive back to her place in Owen's car was a blur. She'd had a couple of glasses of wine and felt as if she were floating. It was Owen that gave her that feeling, not what she'd drank. The wine colored her world, painting it a soft pink and carrying away any problems or logical thoughts that might invade her peace.

"What are you thinking?" Owen asked as they rode up in the elevator.

"I can't tell you." Her head was on his shoulder and she leaned back, smiling up at him. He gazed at her for a moment, then dropped his mouth to meet hers.

"Are they good thoughts?" he muttered against her lips.

"The best." Stephanie held onto the end of the word, sliding her arm up his chest and moving around to fit herself into his body. She kept her mouth on his. Owen deepened the kiss, pulling her tightly against him. Stephanie could feel a moan bubbling up inside her. She didn't try to stop it. She felt too good. It was prom night, graduation, her first date, all rolled into one.

"I want to know what they are."

"What?" Stephanie had forgotten his question. His mouth did things to her body and her mind, like removing all analytical thought and only allowing it to concentrate on the pleasure centers.

"What your thoughts were about."

At her door Stephanie found her key. She slipped it in the lock, the grooves sliding together as the tumblers in the mechanism found their perfect match and joined. She heard the familiar click and opened the door, saving herself from having to answer Owen's question.

Her thoughts were on him, on fantasies—sexual fantasies that involved the two of them and a set of sun-dried sheets. Taking Owen's hand she led him inside. He looked around and Stephanie was aware that he was assessing the place, using his architect's eye to check room proportions and balanced fixtures.

"This is beautiful," he said, turning around. "It looks like you."

Had he known her long enough to know that this is who she was? Stephanie Hunter needed roots. She's been searching for them all her life, sometimes unconsciously. While she'd grown up in a house with her aunt, uncle, and brothers, somehow she had never felt as if it were *her* home. She wanted a house with a yard, a place to have barbecues and summer parties. She'd lived in a house all her life, and had bought one after her salary had gone up while she worked for Josh, but she'd sold it and moved into the cramped space of a condominium apartment to devote her finances to getting her business up and running.

She'd been meticulous with the decoration, using the effects of color, light, and mirrors to make the place appear larger. She was satisfied with the outcome and comfortable with her surroundings, but there were times she missed the cavernous house with its huge rooms and spacious closets. Stephanie had made a commitment to her business. Until she got it solidly on its feet, she had to make sacrifices and living in the apartment was one of them.

"Please, sit down." She offered a huge overstuffed chair designed for two. Emilie claimed it as her own whenever she was there, tucking her feet under her and lying across the entire surface. Stephanie thought the place was intimate, cozy, and warm. That had been her intention with the mauve and muted green colors that comprised the room, but it wasn't the space she wanted for herself.

Owen didn't appear interested in the décor any longer. He was looking at her, staring, openly fixated on her, as if he needed to commit her to memory. They hadn't turned any lights on beyond the solitary one Stephanie had left as a nightlight. She hated returning to a dark space. The lack of illumination made the space close and inviting, intimate as if it were the perfect setting for them. The air was electrified. Stephanie could feel its pulses tapping along her skin like tiny pins vibrating back and forth. The pins touched her nerves, making her throat dry and forcing her to swallow, lick her lips.

Light brightened in Owen's eyes. She didn't know who moved first or how long they took to cross the open space between them, but suddenly Owen was standing in front of her. He was close enough that she could feel the heat from his body. With deliberate slow movements, he captured her face in his hands. Again Stephanie submitted to the scrutiny of his eyes. This time they were full of passion, deep with need and hunger.

Her insides turned to mush. Her skin burned,

hot from the inside out. She wanted Owen like she couldn't remember ever wanting a man. She'd denied it to herself, but her mind and body knew better. She wanted him like she wanted to continue breathing. He slanted his mouth over hers, pushing his tongue inside and delivering truth to fantasies she'd indulged in the darkness of her bedroom. Only this was real. It was better than a fantasy. Time and again he lifted his mouth and repositioned it. Each breaking and entering a live wire dancing and sparking the ground as opposites attracted. A combination pleasure-pain fissured through her, an explosion of nuclear proportion.

Owen's hands massaged her back, working their way from her waist down her hips. Stephanie's breath caught in her throat, then came in quick pants. Her body exploded with need as the dam of emotion within her suddenly burst free. She clung to him as if she'd drown in the rushing water without his assistance. Owen's body was an imprint through her chiffon gown. His arousal was strong and hard against her legs. She liked the feel of him, the way he turned her to a thick liquid that wanted to cover him over. She wanted him closer, wanted their clothes gone, wanted nothing between them but the dermal layer that kept her liquefied insides from spilling onto the floor.

She heard the zipper of her dress make a rasping sound as the teeth separated and the electrified air rushed in to needle her back, finding new erogenous zones. Stephanie moaned as Owen's fingers touched bare skin. Her neck lost its ability to hold her head straight. It fell onto Owen's shoulder. His open mouth kissed her skin, leaving wet spots that sizzled in her ears. She clung to him, barely able to breathe. Heat vibrated around them. Flames licked at her feet, up her calves, around her hips and into the core of her body. If Owen kept this up they'd both dissolve. Or burn into the flames.

Stephanie's dress fell to her feet. Her heightened senses heard the soft rustle of fabric pool around her. Standing in her red bra and lace panties, Owen covered her with his hands, rubbing them up and down her frame, making her hotter than she already was, hotter than she thought any human body could withstand.

Finally his hands slid down her hips, over her legs and under her knees. In seconds she was airborne, lifted in his arms and completely out of the dress at her feet. A small scream escaped her mouth as she was freed from the floor and carried toward her bedroom. How Owen knew which room, she didn't bother to ask. She circled her arms around his neck and let her tongue play in the curve of his ear.

An audible gasp escaped him and he stumbled against the wall. Stephanie laughed at the effect. In her bedroom, he laid her down and sat next to her. The only light came from the moon. He scooped his hands under her head and lifted her mouth to his. Stephanie felt light, weightless, like she was floating on the surface of a lake, yet she was aware of everything, coming to life after a long and deep sleep. She knew the blood rushing through her veins, the feel of the comforter under her back and legs, the soft way Owen held her as if she were a fine wine that would be bruised if handled too roughly. The electrical impulses fired in her brain and the polar magnetism fit together as if they were two halves of the same whole.

His mouth was magic, black magic. It took her down into the depths of passion, the rhythm of drums that beat in her head, in the movement of their bodies, in the sharing of intimacy and the ultimate level of trust.

Stephanie found the buttons on his shirt. With nervous fingers she pushed them through one by one until she could bury her hands against his heated skin. It was moist and warm and felt like velvet. She leaned forward and kissed his chest, feeling his rapidly beating heart against her tongue. His breath was ragged and heavy. Knowing she affected him gave her added confidence. She pulled the shirt free of his pants and continued her exploration of his torso.

Her tongue circled his flat nipples and the tremble that wracked through him passed into her. Owen's hands threaded through her hair, pulling it free and allowing it to flow over her shoulders. He pulled her head back, keeping her mouth from tantalizing his nipples and looked deep into her eyes.

"That feels so good," he said.

"It does?"

"Yes." At the same moment he unhooked her bra and without straps it fell to her waist. Owen's fingers brushed across her nipples. Stephanie jerked at the sudden spiral of pleasure that coiled through her. Owen continued. Her head fell back and her mouth opened at the ecstasy that overtook her.

It was a good thing Owen pushed her down on the pillows. She could no longer sit up without supporting herself against him. His mouth replaced the hands on her breasts and she couldn't keep still. Going for the belt at his waist, she opened it, then tugged the zipper down over his arousal. He stood and in seconds stripped himself of his clothes. Opening the silver packet from his pocket, he protected them and slipped her lace panties off. They joined his discarded pile of clothes on the floor.

Climbing onto the bed with her, Owen rolled onto his side, aligning himself with her. Stephanie ran her hands up and down his arms, over his back and hips, luxuriating in the feel of his strong muscles, unable to contain any form of control. Owen was smooth and warm and she wanted nothing more than to continue her exploration. Pushing her to her back, Owen moved onto her, parted her legs and joined his powerful body with hers.

Stephanie's eyes rolled back in her head and her limbs became a formless liquid. Rapture so delectable it should be bottled and sold at an exorbitant price took control of her being. She bit her lip to keep from screaming at the rapture that filled her.

Owen fit her. The two fit each other. The gentle rock and roll of their bodies took on a life of its own. Each movement thrust him deep within her causing surges of pleasure. Owen took the lead, but she was right there with him. Within seconds their timing escalated. She couldn't get her fill of him. She clung, wrapped her legs around him and allowed a deep and long moan to escape and his body dug deeper into hers.

All she could think of was fire. Together they could create it. Their bodies worked incessantly, generating heat so hot, she knew she'd explode in the created firestorm. Yet she couldn't stop, didn't want to stop. What she felt was so good, too good, no one should be able to withstand this kind of rapture.

Owen was with her, totally with her. They complemented each other, his body well inside hers, his mouth finding hers, his arms enclosing her, and his shouts mingled with her screams. The two of them found the zenith of pleasure coming together in a climax so complete that she felt they couldn't withstand the free fall.

They fell to earth on a dewy cloud of air that cushioned them. Breath came hard, their chests rising and falling against each other. Stephanie tried to control hers, tried to remember a time when she'd felt like this, tried to come to terms with what had happened to her, but her brain wouldn't work. Her body was on pleasure mode and all she could think of was that where she had gone with Owen was a totally new universe. There was no place like it. The two of them had created it alone and only they could find it again.

Owen rolled on his back taking her with him. She lay on top of him, her hair spilling around them. Owen brushed it back and held her against him. His hands, which were big and strong, touched her with all the delicacy of someone holding a newborn baby. Stephanie was cocooned in an aura of guardianship like none she'd ever experienced.

Words weren't necessary to explain what had happened to them. Stephanie wasn't sure she would have been able to express her feelings at this moment if she had to. She closed her eyes and allowed her mind to drift away as her body cooled to the air around them and life was as perfect as it would ever be.

Stephanie woke with a jerk. She'd had a bad dream. Her knee came in contact with a warm body. Looking over she remembered Owen. How could she forget he was there after the night they'd had together? He lay sleeping next to her.

Sometime during the night she'd slid off him and lay cradled in his arms. She wanted to smile, wanted to feel as if this is what she wanted to happen to her all the mornings of her life, but the dream was bright and full and still in her consciousness.

She slid her feet off the bed and stood up. Owen didn't move. Staring at their entwined clothes on the floor, she stepped over them and went to the closet where she took a long robe and covered her nakedness. Then barefoot, she padded to the kitchen and poured herself a beer glass of orange juice.

The sun had barely risen and the there was a fog over the city in the distance. Stephanie stepped out onto the balcony of her apartment and let the cool morning air touch her. There was a slight breeze that lifted her hair. She loved this time of day, before the sun baked and cracked the ground, burned skin to second degrees and before the need to ramp up air-conditioning to the highest levels.

This morning Owen was in her bed. Her body flushed at the thought. She should be there cuddling next to him, but her dream disturbed her. Like an omen appearing to warn her of the coming doom, the dream had been about the Claytons. They were chasing her through various places, her apartment, the offices at the *Dallas Herald*, the dining room at Owen's house. She ran, panting hard and trying to get away from them, while Owen sat at the table and did nothing to help her.

"Good morning." Owen's voice was smooth as brandy, yet it startled Stephanie. She jumped at the sound and the arms that slid around her from the back. She'd been concentrating so hard on the dream that she hadn't heard him.

"Sorry, I didn't mean to scare you." Owen moved around to the front of her. Unconsciously she pulled the robe closer around her. Owen straightened and leaned against the balcony balustrade. "Those thoughts look like they're worth a dollar," he said seriously. "Morning after regrets?"

She shook her head. Last night had been life-altering. She regretted it only in the way it related to the sunlit world. Magic had happened in her bedroom, but they were outside now. The full light of day was only moments away and the harshness of the real world would intrude on their idyllic paradise—and there was no way she could prevent it.

"What is it, then?"

"I had a dream. A bad dream."

"Do you believe in dream analysis? That they control our lives as a predictor of events to come?"

"I never have before."

"Before? Meaning you do now?"

She couldn't answer that positively. There were too many things she didn't know. Her emotions were riding just below her skin and she knew she wanted Owen in her life. But the bonds of familial loyalty were stronger than gravity holding the solar system together. Last night they'd pushed those boundaries, created their own galaxy, but today this one was back in place. They were on earth, not floating somewhere above the stratosphere.

Owen pushed away from the balcony wall and hunkered down next to her. "Tell me about the dream. Was I in it?"

She explained it, speaking as detached as she could. Owen listened without interrupting or reacting. When she finished he took her hand in his and said, "Stephanie, they don't dislike you."

"Then why do I feel as if they do? Why do I feel as if you all know a joke and I'm the butt of it?"

"What?"

"It's nothing I can point to and say it was this or that." She was getting angry, angry with herself, and her voice was rising. Taking a deep breath, she spoke in a more normal tone. "It's the way I'm looked at, the inflection in voices when I'm asked a question. They're searching for something and if I have it, I don't know it."

"Stephanie, you had a dream. That is not reality."

"I know that. I know that dreams are a manifestation of things that happen to you during the day. It's the brain's way of dealing with issues. In my life, this is an issue. *You* are an issue." She paused, thinking about whether she wanted to tell Owen how completely last night had changed her. She decided to take the plunge. Her heart was already lost. If he rejected her at least she would know. "Last night I told you I was attracted to you. It goes deeper than that. A lot deeper. I know you aren't one for staying, for committing to anyone, but last night, in there" —she nodded toward the bedroom— "I felt as if the world belonged to us."

Owen stood up, pulling her to her feet. He drew her into his arms and kissed her forehead.

"It did," he said.

Chapter Nine

Stephanie read the note again. Tears welled up in her eyes, but she smiled through them. It was her first genuine smile in days. The note was from Josh and was accompanied by a check for more than the bank loan she'd applied for. Josh had rescued her and she would pay him back with more than money. They might have different firms and her loan was strictly business on the surface, with papers, installment payments, due dates, and interest rates, but whenever Josh needed her to be there for him, she would be there.

He was her last source when the bank turned her down. The *Dallas Herald* job would put her on her feet, but she had to finish it before she'd be able to walk with ease. And there were other requests for her services coming in every day. Word was getting around. A piece about Rusty Shulman's offices was in the Arts section of the *Herald*. The television show had begun to air her programs and mail from that was pouring in. The cable studio sent it to her. Marian couldn't handle it, but with the check from Josh, Stephanie could hire a design student to do the mail and to help with other jobs.

She should be happy. Everything she'd worked for was falling in place. Owen was the only wild card marring an otherwise perfect plan. He'd consoled her the morning after. Held her in his arms and said all the pretty words, but he hadn't been able to remove her opinion of the Claytons.

"You're going to be late," Marian said, coming into Stephanie's office.

Stephanie looked up, confused. "Oh," she said, jumping up from her chair. She had an appointment with John Addison, publisher of the *Dallas Herald* to go over his office design. Stuffing the check in her purse, she headed for the door. She could deposit it after her meeting.

"Don't forget this," Marian reminded her, pointing to the storyboards and room layout Stephanie had meticulously prepared. Some people couldn't envision paint or fabric from small swatches as it would look when covering a wall or windows. Since John Addison had only a little time, she figured a picture would be worth a twenty minute discussion.

"Remember you also have that interview tonight." Marian held the door as Stephanie angled the large box reminiscent of past science projects out to her SUV and climbed into the driver's seat. Marian smiled at her from the door. As Stephanie drove away, she mentally went over her daybook entries. After her appointment with John Addison, she was meeting with a reporter doing a story on her and the television program. The station had set it up. They thought it would be good publicity for the program.

She arrived at the currently occupied offices of the *Dallas Herald* with ten minutes to spare. Addison saw her on time and an hour later she was laughing as she left his office. The meeting went well. She knew him better now, knew what he liked and disliked about his current office, knew that he loved sunlight, but it often caused a glare. Stephanie suggested something called an invisible screen for the windows. It was a screen of shade cloth that could be raised and lowered by a button on his desk console. He could adjust the brightness or raise it completely and invisibly under a cornice she'd design. From there the meeting produced very positive suggestions. He liked the suggested color schemes, which would make the room warm and inviting, but be a place conducive to work. He was allergic to pollen and preferred plants that did not aggravate him.

With a smile and a handshake, Stephanie left him to his next appointment, which was with Seymour Worth, director of circulation. He introduced Stephanie as she had an appointment with him the next day.

Stephanie was humming when she reached her SUV. She got inside the stiflingly hot space and pulled her cell phone out. Maybe Emilie was available for a late lunch. She wasn't. In fact, she was too busy to come to the phone. The hospital sounded as if it was in turmoil. She tried Josh, but he had Megan Sikking to deal with and she was always time consuming. Stephanie thanked him for the check, understood about Mrs. Sikking and got off the phone. Megan Sikking spent an obscene amount of money on decorating, but she was a card to work for. Josh handled her well, treating her as if she were a queen. That was exactly what she wanted and she returned to him frequently.

Hanging up, Stephanie started the SUV and decided to have lunch alone. Turning out of the parking lot, she decided she wouldn't go to Jake's. There was every likelihood that she could run into Owen there and she wasn't taking the chance of that happening. It had been three days since they'd made love and Stephanie could still remember the imprint of his body against hers, the feel his mouth on hers and the tantalizing way he had of brushing his thumbs over her nipples.

"Oh," she gasped, as mind and body coincided and she nearly ran into the oncoming lane. Safely concentrating on her driving, the Margharita House came to mind. She would have lunch there. The food was Mexican and good, the drinks were a specially made and delicious concoction of Margharita's. Stephanie was driving and had a full afternoon of work to get done. She would have a diet cola, but the real draw of the Margharita House was its freedom from the Claytons.

Stephanie was wrong. As soon as the waiter showed her to a table, Rosa Clayton appeared in front of her.

"Hi," Rosa said.

Stephanie smiled in spite of herself. "Hello."

"Are you alone?"

"Yes, I was just going to get something quick. I have errands to run this afternoon."

"So do I. Would you mind if I joined you?"

Stephanie gestured with her hand for the younger woman to sit down. Rosa pulled out the chair and sat down. The maitre 'd handed each of them a brightly colored menu that was as large as a wall portrait.

"I thought you had gone back to your modeling job. Sweden, wasn't it?" Stephanie couldn't remember which country she'd flown in from the night of the dinner.

"It was, but the shoot ended and I jumped on the first plane back here."

"Don't you live in New York?"

"I have an apartment there."

Stephanie looked over her menu. Rosa was hidden behind hers. Stephanie wondered if it had anything to do with the stares coming from every male in the room.

"But you flew here. Why?"

She put the menu down and looked at Stephanie. "I wanted to talk to you."

"How did you know I'd be here?"

"I followed you."

Stephanie laughed. She expected Rosa to do the same, but Owen's beautiful model sister kept her face straight.

"You really followed me? I thought that was a joke."

"I came by the office, but got there in time to see you drive away."

"I was at the *Herald* for an hour. You weren't waiting all that time?"

"I have some friends there I went to school with. I talked to them until you came down."

"Why didn't you just call me?"

"Fear of rejection." She paused. "I want to apologize for the night we met and for the dinner party."

"Did Owen ask you to do this?"

"He doesn't know I'm in town. I've been at the house for two days, but he hasn't been there."

Stephanie wondered where he was. Was he sick somewhere? Had he had an accident and no one knew about it? He could have amnesia. Multiple horrors went through her mind.

"I talked to his secretary. He's at one of the sites.

Apparently things aren't going well and he has to be there for several days."

Stephanie pulled the menu up to cover her face and closed her eyes in relief.

"Have you ladies decided?" Stephanie was surprised to find the waiter standing next to her. She hadn't looked at the menu at all. Falling back on the standard, she ordered a taco salad. Rosa ordered the same.

When he left, Rosa began. "The night at the art gallery I was in a mood. It had nothing to do with you, but I took my frustration out on you. I want to apologize for that. And the family dinner. You looked overwhelmed and we asked a lot of questions. Told stories you probably didn't understand. I felt you were uncomfortable and I did nothing to relieve that. But I want to make up for it."

"Apology accepted," Stephanie said. She was also suspicious now. She couldn't help thinking there was something more in Rosa's presence. What was it the Claytons wanted from her?

"I mean it," Rosa said. "I want us to be friends. I don't have many friends, at least, not women." She looked about the room, encompassing the stares as her reason. Stephanie understood. It must be hard being so beautiful. Men wanted you and women hated you. "And Owen seems to have a thing for you."

There is was, Stephanie thought, that undercurrent of something else driving this apology.

"Owen has a thing for a lot of women," Stephanie said. It was no secret. She wanted Rosa to know she was aware of her brother's reputation with women.

"He's never seemed as *interested* in any of them the way he's interested in you."

Thoughts of their one passionate night together

came to her, but she said, "You want to be friends with me because of your brother?"

"We're a very close family."

"Family. That's quickly becoming a four letter word."

"What?"

"You all say it," Stephanie told her. "You seem to want to make sure that I know you're a family. I get it. I get it that you're the Claytons and I am not."

"Stephanie, I didn't mean it like that."

"Then how did you mean it? What is it about the group of you that is trying so hard? What happened? Is there a fortune left by Reuben and Devon and you want to cut me out of it?" Rosa gasped as if Stephanie had delivered her a blow. "Well, I don't need it," she lied. "I was perfectly content with my life before I met you Claytons." Stephanie stood up and dropped her napkin on the table. "You can all go back to your family meetings and secret codes, to pushing people who only want to be friends and make them feel like outsiders. I don't need you."

Stephanie left. She wanted to make a theatrical exit, but her aunt had drummed manners into her. Even if the woman never approved of anything Stephanie did, manners were part of her makeup. Stephanie walked slowly to the door and out into the glaring sunshine. She welcomed it. It felt good on her face and arms, as if she'd left a dark cavern and entered the world of air and light.

No longer hungry, but with her stomach churning, Stephanie returned to the office. Fifteen minutes later she heard someone come in. Looking up she saw Rosa leaning against the doorjamb. The beautiful young woman held up a bag with the Margharita House logo on it.

"I'm going to get this out one way or another."
Stepping through the door, she kicked it closed.

Stephanie had been angry. Very angry. But the
fight went out of her when she realized that one of
the most beautiful women on the planet wanted to
apologize to her. She laughed, a deep belly laugh
that expunged all the negative feelings she'd held
inside.

"It's my turn to apologize," Stephanie said. "It
wasn't you, either. I had someone else on my mind
and you got the brunt of my anger."

"Owen?" she asked.

"How did you know?" Stephanie decided to tell
the truth.

"We're fam—" She stopped in mid-sentence.
Again, they both laughed.

Over the meal Rosa told her the stories
Stephanie had thought Owen would tell her; what
it was like growing up with Devon and Reuben
Clayton as parents. She envied them their wonderful times, their holidays and the closeness they had
with each other. Stephanie was close to her brothers. She had grand memories of her uncle and
brothers, weekends camping or swimming in
wooded lakes. She didn't live in the warm cocoon
of unconditional love, but she hadn't had a bad
life.

She wished life had been different, but she
couldn't go back and change it and wishing didn't
help anything. If life had been different where
would the Clayton children be today? Would Owen
and Brad have died on the streets long ago? How
long would Digger have lived stealing food and
sleeping in railroad cars? Would he have lost a leg
or been killed under one of those cars one night
when he was running and fell? And what of Digger
and Erin? Would she have ever met them? Would

she have the memories of Owen's body so intimately joined to hers? Yes, she envied these Claytons finding her parents, but without those loving parents to guide and love them, this family, who were only together by happenstance, might be far different today.

"Thank you, Rosa," Stephanie said when silence grew between them.

"For what?"

"For being persistent, for telling me about my parents, for being my new friend."

When Stephanie looked over there were tears in Rosa's eyes.

Stephanie felt a pang of remorse at believing there was an ulterior motive in Rosa befriending her. Either the young woman was an extremely good actress or she genuinely wanted to be friends. It was a new friendship, one that wasn't ready for a test yet. Stephanie wanted to ask her a question, but decided to wait. She wanted to know what it was they were hiding from her.

Owen hadn't expected to have to spend the night in Tyler. He'd taken nothing with him, but swung the backpack he'd bought to carry the clothes and toiletries he'd needed for his three days away, on the bed in his bedroom. He'd wanted to drive straight to Stephanie's apartment, but needed a shower and time to calm down. He'd thought of nothing but her for three nights, and knowing he was on his way to her, the entire drive had played like a mantra in his head of getting to Stephanie.

Owen turned on the water and stripped. He stepped under the spray and closed the glass door. The feelings he had for Stephanie were new. They

spiraled out of control at the slightest thought.
During his three days all he could think of was
their night together, the passionate embraces and
how he wanted to hold her, wake with her, make
plans with her, and share many more nights finding the same nirvana.

The hot water beat at his tired muscles, washing
away the tightness, the road wear, replacing it with
a clean feeling that comes from using your own
personal space. He could reach out and find his
soap without looking to see if it were there. He
knew where it was, as much as a piano player
knows key spans without looking at his hands.

He wondered about Stephanie. He'd called her
several times, but got no answer. When he tried
her office she was always out. Marian had delivered the same message to him so often he was beginning to wonder if the woman was avoiding him.
But why would she?

He knew she didn't think she fit in with his family. And he'd be a liar if he didn't think that mattered to him. He wanted her to like them and they
to like her. But her perception didn't come from
nothing. Rosa wasn't hospitable when they first
met. And when he looked back at the dinner party,
he could see how all of them could be overwhelming. He compared her to his two sisters-in-law. Erin
hadn't seemed to mind when Digger brought her
the first time. Mallory was buffeted by distance, yet
since she'd married Brad she'd been easily en-
folded in the group as if she were one of them.
Mallory also had the shared experience of losing
her parents early in life.

Owen was going to have to confront the issue,
but not with a family meeting. Maybe it would be
better to let her get to know them one at a time.

Taking a moment to call Stephanie after he was

dressed and receiving the same answering machine message, Owen consulted his watch as he strapped it on his arm. He decided that even though it was late she was probably at the construction site.

It didn't take him long to find her. She was on the top floor, in the executive offices. Surrounding her were carpet samples, wallpaper rolls, paint wheels. She had a tape measure around her neck and a myriad of measuring tools next to her feet. For a moment Owen stood and watched her. He loved the way she moved. She wore a tan colored pantsuit with strappy sandals.

As if sensing she was being watched, she turned around.

"Owen," she said, his name a breath on her lips. He loved the way she said it.

"I missed you," he said, opening his arms. Her mouth lifted into a big smile. She ran to him. Owen caught her and swung her around. For a moment he was afraid she'd back away from him. But she was his. He set her down and took her mouth. He had missed her terribly.

"Why didn't you answer my phone calls?" He asked his question through several kisses, then took her mouth in a hungry exchange, not giving her time to answer. "Didn't you know it was driving me crazy?" Owen was surprised he'd said that. Never had he let a woman know she'd gotten under his skin.

"I didn't know you'd gone until Rosa told me."

"Rosa?"

"We had lunch yesterday." Owen's arms went slack and Stephanie stepped out of them. "It didn't start off well, but we mended the fences. I think she's a great person and for one so young, she has a lot of sense."

"Wow, maybe I should leave town more often."

"I hope not."

His heart lurched when she said that. "It's strange that Rosa would come here. I was thinking that maybe you should meet the family one by one instead of as a group. I guess Rosa had the same thought."

"She really is concerned for you and wants only the best. Apparently she feels you need looking after."

Early in Rosa's life she idolized Owen. She used to follow him around, getting knocked down if he turned around too fast. She'd laugh each time it happened and raise her tiny arms for him to lift her up. It made sense that she would be especially interested in his well-being. He'd explained to her more than once that he liked his life as it was, but Rosa continually tried to pester him into settling down and finding someone special.

It was ironic that when Owen did find someone who stood out from the crowd, his sister didn't really take to her. That is, until this week and her seeking out Stephanie for lunch.

"Are you going to be here much longer?" Owen knew he hadn't responded to Stephanie's statement. He'd been close to telling her he wanted her to look after him, but saying that was too much like a proposal. Something in him stopped his words. He'd cautioned himself so long it had become habit. But still he knew he wasn't ready for marriage.

"I'm about finished."

"Good. Let's go to Jake's."

Owen helped Stephanie pack her things. She told him about her lunch with his sister while she put her samples in their appropriate storage units. Then they took the caged elevator to the bottom floor and out to the SUV. Leaving it parked, he drove them to the white table cloth and rosebud establishment and was immediately shown to a table.

It was early for a crowd. By nine o'clock there would be people waiting at the bar and outside in the garden area that had been designed for just such occasions. For seven o'clock there were a good number of people at the tables. Needless to say, he knew more than a few of them.

While he wanted to talk to Stephanie, people kept stopping by to speak to him. "Owen, I've been meaning to talk to you. Give me a call later this week," Jack Currey said, shaking his hand. That's the way most of the greetings went. But then a couple of women smiled and waved from nearby tables. He looked at Stephanie, who commented, but appeared amused.

"Owen, where have you been?" Amanda Strickler came up behind him. When he turned in his chair she dropped a kiss on his cheek. "And why haven't you called me?"

"Amanda, I thought you were out of town, Georgia wasn't it?"

"It didn't work out." She said it as if she were ready to pick up things where they'd left off when she'd moved away after they stopped seeing each other.

Owen introduced her to Stephanie, who offered her hand. The two women shook, but Amanda immediately dismissed Stephanie's presence and continued talking to him.

After a minute or so she left, promising him they would get together soon.

"She's very pretty," Stephanie said when she was gone. "I supposed this would happen sooner or later," Stephanie said.

"What would happen?"

"Your love life coming back to haunt you . . . if it's coming back." She added the last as if he were currently in a relationship with Amanda.

"I haven't seen her in months." He defended himself. "It's not like I have women coming out of the walls." There was a time he'd be proud to be able to say he did have that many women, but no longer. He wanted Stephanie to believe him.

"Not the walls." She nodded behind him. Owen turned. He had to force himself not to let his face fall when he saw Merle McCormack rushing across the room. Owen stood and she propelled herself into his arms.

"I was hoping to see you here tonight. How have you been?"

"Fine. Busy."

"Yes, I've been reading about you in the newspaper."

Owen took a moment to introduce Stephanie.

"Hello." Merle shook hands with Stephanie. "Haven't I seen you before?" Then answering her own question, she said, "You're doing that interior design TV show. My mother loves it."

Stephanie's expression wasn't lost on Owen, although Merle had turned back to him. It was a backhanded insult.

"Well, I'd better get back to my date. You remember Travis Payne." She lowered her voice to a conspiratorial tone. "You know how jealous he can be. Call me some time. We need to get back together." Then glancing at Stephanie, she said, "Nice meeting you, Stella."

Like a flighty bird Merle was moving back the way she had come.

"I apologize," he said, reseating himself.

"Not so fast," Stephanie stopped him. "Here comes another one."

Owen barely had time to turn in his chair before there was a woman on his lap. Cheryl Moore had her arms around his neck and her mouth on his. How could this be happening? How could three of the most demonstrative women he'd ever met be in the same place at the same time? If he didn't know better he'd think this was a practical joke fostered by his brothers, but they didn't know he would be at Jake's tonight and none of them were in town.

"Cheryl." He pulled her arms from around his neck and his mouth from hers. "What are you doing?"

"I missed you," she said.

"The last I heard you were getting married."

"I couldn't. I got all the way to the bridal shower and I knew I couldn't marry Eddie. He's a nice guy, but he's not you." She tried to kiss him again. Owen restrained her.

"Cheryl, I have a date."

Cheryl looked around. "Not anymore. That's great. Now we can spend the night together."

Owen stood up, forcing Cheryl to her feet. Where had Stephanie gone? He looked toward the exit. She was nowhere to be seen. He rushed out of the restaurant looking for her. She was gone as if she'd evaporated into thin air. She had no car, yet she'd eluded him.

"Damn," he cursed, punching his fist into his hand. He'd thought the day would be one for the memory books. And it was. Maybe in years to come he'd look back on it and laugh at the way things had gone tonight, but right now he wanted to click his fingers and make it all disappear.

* * *

Stephanie had never been so humiliated in her life. She hopped into a taxi at the entrance and had it drive her back to her SUV. Unsure if Owen would extricate himself from the sex-pot on his lap long enough to notice she was gone, or follow her, had her feeling numb. She wanted to be with him, but she knew his reputation. Tonight it had been driven home to her. Owen Clayton was a virile man. She knew that from firsthand experience. Unfortunately, she wasn't the only woman in Dallas who knew it.

Or wanted it to continue.

She got in the SUV and quickly fired the engine, exiting the parking lot right behind the taxi that had dropped her off. She didn't want to face Owen even if he did come after her.

Life would be so much easier if she hadn't been so curious about the Claytons. She wouldn't have the contract for the *Dallas Herald* and she wouldn't be in love with him.

Stephanie stopped the SUV at a red light. She hadn't been looking where she was going. She should be headed for her apartment, but she was actually going in the opposite direction.

How could she be in love with Owen Clayton? He was nothing like the man of her dreams, the one she'd conjured up in her head as the ideal mate. She'd never choose a Casanova as someone she wanted to spend her life with. Owen was tall and handsome, the perfect long drink of water she envisioned, but he was also mysterious. He was charming, passionate, and caring and when he held her in his arms she felt like she was the only woman in the world.

A horn blew behind her and she quickly switched

on a signal and turned right, backtracking her way and heading home. Parking in the underground garage, she took the elevator to her lobby and crossed it to the bank leading to the living floors. Owen stood in the hallway waiting for her.

He pushed away from the door the moment the elevator doors opened. "I'm sorry," he said. He looked as if the world had been dropped on him. "I never expected—"

"What? That women would throw themselves at you?"

Stephanie got out of the small room as the door began to close. Her key was already in her hand. She didn't want to talk to him tonight, but the confrontation had to happen sometime. It might as well be now. She opened the door and preceded him inside.

"I didn't know they would show up tonight or act the way they did."

"It's all right," she spoke calmly. "It had to end sometime. Better now than when we're emotionally invested in each other." She knew it was already too late for that, but pride made her say it.

Stephanie turned as if the discussion was over.

"What?" Owen shouted. "Is that how you react? You run? Give up? As if nothing happened between us?"

"No, Owen, that is how *you* react. Things get hot, too complicated, she wants more out of the relationship and *you* end it. I'm just saving you the trouble."

"I don't believe you. You couldn't fake what happened the other night."

Stephanie could tell he was angry. "I didn't fake it. But neither am I going to allow a night in bed with you to change my life."

She walked further away from him, mainly because she couldn't stand the look on his face. Knowing she put it there was even worse. She stood near the balcony door and turned around.

"Owen, we made a pact that we never lived up to. That was a mistake. I can't end the contract so I'm bound to see you, but let's put things back on a business level. It's only when we get personal that things get out of hand."

"Is that what you really want?"

No, no, her mind screamed. But she nodded her head.

"I can explain those women . . ."

"You're missing the point," she interrupted. "It's not about those women. Owen, I'd be a fool if I didn't think you'd lived a normal life to this point. But your lifestyle and mine don't mix."

"And you feel that there isn't a meeting place for us?"

"Do you really want an *us*? Or is your ego bruised a little because you aren't the one initiating the end?"

Stephanie had had enough relationships to know that men didn't do well when women broke up with them.

"This isn't about my ego."

"What is it about then?"

He came toward her, his stride as smooth and even as a black panther. Stephanie wanted to run. She knew she should run. Somewhere inside her the element of self-preservation reared its logical head, but she couldn't find the logical track. She was too busy trying to determine Owen's actions. She stood her ground.

"This is what it's about." Before she could evade him, Owen had his arms around her waist and his mouth on hers. Stephanie's arms came up to grab him and push him away, but the magic was already working. It entered her blood like a narcotic. Her arms hung upward like a garden statue, her mind fighting the battle of her emotions. Emotions won and she joined Owen in the kiss, relaxing her body and allowing feeling to roll over her in waves of passion. His mouth devoured her, his tongue invading like an army on the move. He wasn't holding her as if she were delicate, but as if he needed to brand her with his own personal logo.

Stephanie accepted the brand, one of her legs climbing over Owen's, entwining them together. He moved his hands down her body, clutching her hips and grinding them into his arousal. Stephanie moaned. All the new love she'd discovered within her transmitted itself to Owen. Her arms circled his neck and for the second time he lifted her.

"Have I ever told you I like being carried?" she said.

"No." His voice held laughter. "But I will be sure to remember it."

Stephanie didn't think it was possible to repeat the wizardry of a few nights ago. She was sure it was witchcraft and that nothing could top what they had found in each other. But Owen proved her wrong. She didn't take time to wonder if her new love for him affected her, but as they hurried to undress and join their bodies, Stephanie knew she couldn't hold back. Not tonight, not when he was doing luscious things with his mouth. Owen protected them and slid effortlessly into her. He was holding her, touching his lips over her hot skin, drawing a river of fire from the never-exhausting furnaces below her skin. She wanted to scream for him to stop, but it felt too good.

His hands covered her skin, finding new areas of delight as they roamed over her breasts, stomach, hips and lower. Stephanie heard her own sexual sounds, panting, long gasping breaths, and pleasure-moans that had her seeking the meaning of life. She didn't want him to stop. She never wanted him to stop. She wanted this assault to her senses, to her very being, to go on as long as life flowed.

Rolling over she topped Owen, her knees cushioned into the soft coverlet. Guiding him with her hand, she took him into her body with a deep thrust. She nearly cried out at the sensations that rioted through her. His long body under hers, hot as a three-alarmer, sweet with sexual sweat, bathed in a room pungent with electrified love, speaking the language of need, want, lust, and love.

Owen took one breast in his mouth and used his hand to tease the nipple of her other as Stephanie hovered over him. Responding to his sensual assault was the final straw. With a mind of its own she rocked over him, her body setting the pace as she took his penis inside her, moving up the length of it and then down again. Each movement touching off millions of nerve endings that found the erogenous areas of the brain and returned with a passion to repeat the assault. Their bodies convulsed. Her inner muscles squeezed him hard. She could hear him groaning in pleasure, holding her tightly, pumping her up and down so she wouldn't stop the sensations. The tide within them moved, its undertow strong, lethal, showing them a jewel they each reached for, wanted, needed and were destined to possess.

Stephanie heard her own scream barely covered by the shout from Owen. They'd reached it, the turbulent point of ecstasy claimed them, held them, let them experience it. For an eternity or a moment they left their physical being and floated in a sea of sensation, rapture, passion. Everything was in superlatives, the greatest, the best, the most, the ultimate. It was a ride like no other and when they reached the point of death, the place where another infinitesimal amount of incomparable passion would destroy them, they fell back to earth.

Stephanie collapsed against Owen.

Spent.

Wet.

Completely satiated.

And totally in love.

The phone was ringing and it was on Owen's side of the bed. Stephanie didn't want to answer it. She was ensconced in a dream world with the man she loved. She had no use for phones. And at this hour.

Lying across Owen, she checked the clock and saw it was just after 5:00 A.M. Only an emergency would have someone calling her at this hour. She immediately thought of her uncle. Had something happened to him?

Jerking herself up, she reached for it, but her arm fell short of the distance needed. Owen lifted the cordless receiver and handed it to her.

"Stephanie, who did you tell you were Cynthia Clayton?"

"What?" Stephanie sat up, pulling the covers with her as if the person on the phone could see her nakedness sprawled across Owen. "Aunt Meriweather?"

Stephanie could count on one finger the number of times her aunt had called her since she moved into the apartment. Even when her uncle was ill, it was one of her brothers who called to let her know. Her brothers and her uncle shortened her aunt's name to Meri, but the older woman insisted that Stephanie address her formally, without any familial endearing of terms.

"Of course, it's me. How many other people know you're really Cynthia Clayton?"

"Aunt Meriweather, I don't understand."

Owen put his hand on her arm. She knew he could feel the tension coiling inside her. And the leashed tone of her voice let him know something was wrong.

"A reporter came by here yesterday. She wanted to know if it was true that you were raised here and that you are the same baby who was kidnapped from Devon and Reuben Clayton thirty-four years ago. She had a picture of you."

"What did you tell her?"

"What did *I* tell her? She didn't get the story from me. She was only here for confirmation."

"And you confirmed it?"

"I did nothing of the kind." She paused. Stephanie could hear her heavy breathing through the telephone line. "I want you to know that you can get this family in a huge amount of trouble if you go telling that story."

"Aunt Meriweather, I didn't. I haven't talked to any report—" She stopped. She had talked to a reporter, but about her television show. She'd said nothing personal beyond her college education and going into the design business.

"Well this woman, this reporter" —she said reporter like it had a bad odor— "she's hunting for a story on you and it doesn't look like she has to go far to find it. You always were more trouble than you were worth."

"You have no right to say . . ." Stephanie heard the click of the receiver. Her aunt had hung up on her.

She handed the phone back to Owen who replaced it on its cradle. "I take it that was the aunt who doesn't like you."

"Meriweather Carter." Stephanie's voice had tears in it. As much as she hated it, the woman still got to her. She waited a moment before speaking. "Somehow a reporter has found out I was kidnapped and went to my aunt for confirmation."

Owen pulled her into the crook of his arm.

"She didn't tell me what paper or magazine it was, when it would run, who has it. Her concern is that I could somehow get *her* in trouble." She ran her arms around Owen's waist. "I could, but I wouldn't. She didn't kidnap me. After my parents died, she took us in, always provided for us and my uncle gave me all the love a child could want. It wasn't the best of households, but it wasn't the worst either. She never beat me. She often said things that hurt me, but I learned to ignore them."

"What are you going to do about the story?"

"I don't know. Several options come to mind. I could go to the police and preempt the story, unless it runs today. I could deny it, but since I went to the Adopted Children's Bureau and left my name and address my lie will be easily discovered. I could run, clean out my bank account and disappear into the fabric of America."

"Which one do you want to do?" Owen asked quietly.

"None of the above. I wanted publicity for my business, because I'm a good decorator. I don't want notoriety. I don't want reporters camping out at my aunt and uncle's house asking them why they never told the truth to the authorities. I don't want my brothers hurt by anything that has to do with me." She sat up and leaned away from him. "But I don't have that luxury, do I?"

"You're a thirty-four year old mystery. That will make people curious, but you won't be on the front page. World news will cover that. Enough people, however, will read the back pages, and through the genius of the Internet the news will be sent to all the people who you know here in Dallas."

"So my choices are one," Stephanie said with a sigh. "I try to preempt the newspaper story."

Owen nodded, agreeing with the decision she had already made. "But, you won't have to do it alone."

"I won't?"

Owen reached for the phone. "This is when you learn the meaning of family."

Chapter Ten

Stephanie was seeing first hand what it was like to have someone in her corner, someone who was looking out for her interest. Owen went into attack mode. Right after they showered and dressed, he began laying out a plan. While he had her phoning the reporter and setting up a press conference, he called his entire family and gave them an update on what had happened. Without a second thought they agreed to stand with her. Stephanie called her brothers and her uncle. They, too, didn't hesitate to be present as soon as she had a date and time.

It didn't take long for them to get things rolling or for reporters to start clambering for the story. Stephanie's phone started to ring as soon as she hung it up.

After the third reporter she told everything would be explained at the meeting, she saw Owen closing his cell phone.

"I have an idea," he said. "Let's get out of here. They can't get us if they can't reach us."

"All right. Where are we going?"

"To visit my mother."

"Your biological mother?"

He nodded. "You know about her?"

"I read a news report about her last year." At the time Stephanie didn't know that the event she was reading about had anything to do with her or her future involvement with the man standing before her.

"That was her on the phone. She's expecting us for lunch."

"What about the police?"

"We'll go there first. I know a few detectives. Hopefully, they'll be done with us before lunch."

"Thank you," Stephanie said. She went to him and kissed him.

"What am I being thanked for?"

"For being a Clayton."

It had been a long day, but by three o'clock every one of the Claytons had arrived in Dallas and Stephanie had had a pleasant lunch with Mariette Randall. She didn't know what to expect of Owen's biological mother, but she was a shy woman with a warm personality. Stephanie liked her instantly, more than she'd liked any of the Claytons.

But her pleasant day was ending. Her stomach was in knots and her hands were clammy and moist. The press conference was scheduled for five and as Stephanie walked into the room at the Renfrew Hotel, she led an army of supporters. In addition to the Claytons, her three brothers were there, Emilie stood next to her on one side, Owen on the other. Simon Thalberg, the detective who'd tracked her, and her uncle Jackson Carter were in attendance. Mariette Randall had come with Owen and Stephanie when they finished their lunch. The only family member absent was Aunt Meriweather. Several policemen and detectives were also present.

Stephanie had spent the morning telling her story. Owen filled in pieces and the clippings they found that started the search were given over to the authorities. Her file from thirty-four years ago was produced, along with the DNA results, forged birth certificates, child photos and those that had been aged to tell what she might look like at various ages. The authorities didn't think there would be much in the way of prosecution, unless Stephanie wished to bring charges.

She didn't.

Lights flashed as cameras immediately began snapping pictures. "I wonder if there is any national news today," she muttered so only Owen could hear her.

He took her arm and guided her to the seat behind all the microphones. Without a real beginning to the proceedings, questions were thrown at her. How do you feel about being found after thirty-four years? When did you find out you were adopted? What do you think of your adoptive parents? What do you think of your kidnapper? They went on and on. Stephanie answered none of them. She waited until the room was quiet, then she began to speak, giving the prepared monologue she'd already memorized.

She told the reporters the story as she knew it, emphasizing that her parents loved her and treated her with all the kindness afforded any child who is loved. She was denied nothing and they were always supportive. When she finished the questions began again. She answered them as best she could.

When they had exhausted questions on her,

they resorted to calling her mother and father her kidnappers. Stephanie hated the reference.

"They were not my kidnappers," she said clearly into the mike. "They were my protectors, my family."

"You think the people who stole you from your real parents are your protectors?" The question was asked by a short man with glasses and a small crop of hair that he combed over his crown.

Owen touched her hand. She looked at him. "You don't have to answer anything you don't want to," he whispered out of mike range.

"I'm all right," she told him.

"Yes, both of them protected me. My parents and my adoptive parents kept me safe and provided for my needs. I always felt love with and for them. And I always will."

"What happened to your real mother?"

"She died."

"And the woman who kidnapped you."

"She died, too."

"Same for your fathers?"

She nodded, then realized she had to speak. "They are all dead now."

"So you've lost your entire family?" Again the bad comb-over spoke.

"This is my family." Stephanie spread her hands to encompass the people behind her. "These are the children the Claytons adopted. These are my brothers." She didn't say stepbrothers or adoptive brothers because that is not how she thought of them or how they thought of her. "This is my Uncle Jack. And this is my best friend, Emilie. Many of them have traveled great distances to get here. So you see, I have a lot of family."

"What about the money?"

Stephanie looked to see where that question

had come from. In the corner stood the reporter who'd interviewed her a little more than a week ago. She also noticed a look pass between Rosa and Dean. They took a step closer to her and she relaxed, thinking they were coming to her rescue should she need them.

"What money?"

"Well, your biological parents left a house and a little money. This went to their adoptive children, but according to the law, you're entitled to some of it."

"I have no desire to contest the terms of their wills or the settlement of the estate."

When the group began shouting other questions at her—How much money did they leave? How much is the house worth? Was she independently wealthy?—Stephanie heard the word "follow-up" from the reporter in the corner. The room quieted for the woman's next question. "The will is all fine and good, but what about the thirty-four year old bank account?"

This time she was sure of what she saw passing between the Clayton siblings.

"Where did you find out about that?" Owen asked, leaning over to speak. Stephanie wanted to turn and stare at him, but she knew she was on camera and didn't want it to appear that she was totally surprised by Owen's apparent knowledge.

Which she was.

"According to bank records, your parents—the biological ones—" she added, "set up a bank account from donations when you were kidnapped. It's been gathering interest for thirty-four years."

A murmur went through the room.

"Bank records are private." Owen's tone was accusing.

"I broke no laws obtaining the information. It

was printed in the paper as a dormant account ten years ago. I suppose Ms. Clayton's real parents forgot about it. Later it was revived."

"How much is it worth now?" someone shouted. Stephanie didn't look to see where the question had come from. Her mind was trying to wrap itself around the fact that Owen knew about it and hadn't told her.

"Four million dollars and change."

"What?" Stephanie spoke before she knew she'd said anything. She had four million dollars. She'd been turned down by the bank for a loan, had borrowed money from a friend and all the while she was sitting on a fortune.

"What are you going to do with all that money?"

Stephanie looked at the reporter. "I haven't decided," she said.

Stephanie couldn't take it any longer. She answered a few more questions then stood up to leave. "I believe you have enough for a story. Thank you."

"What about the television show?" The shout came from the back of the room. More questions were thrown at her. So many that she couldn't hear any of them clearly. Her entourage moved like a wave shielding her from the cameras and the questions. In the hall, Owen shepherded her to a back elevator and up to a suite where they'd gathered before going down to face the press.

Now she had to face the family.

Preceding everyone into the suite, Stephanie walked all the way across the room to the windows of the high-rise hotel. Her brothers followed her. As soon as the door closed she turned to look at the inhabitants of the room. Her shoulders shook with anger. Seeing Owen approaching her, she stopped him with the dark rage that was in her eyes. Like a family feuding, the Claytons faced her and her brothers stood behind her. Simon Thalberg, Emilie and her uncle stood to the side behind a large dining room table that had been laden with food.

"Stephanie, are you all right?" Owen took a step toward her.

She moved back, standing on a line with her three silent brothers. "Don't come near me." She extended her arm, palm out and pronounced each venom-covered word separately.

Owen stopped, an expression on his face that mirrored someone who'd just taken a bullet to the chest.

"Is this your idea of family?" She included the entire clan, sweeping them with eyes as lethal as flying daggers. "You all knew, didn't you? My entire life has been investigated, scrutinized, tested, and opened like a book. You know everything about me, my business, my finances, everything down to my DNA chains, but to you I'm the dirty little secret."

She brought her gaze back to Owen. She might be able to ignore the other family members. They were all absent participants, but Owen was here, intimately vested in the deception that had her learning she had a bank account.

"Stephanie, let me explain." Owen spoke. She jerked as if a hot poker had touched her arm.

"Isn't it time you stopped explaining, stopped lying?" She shook her head from side to side. "Oh, you're good. Perfect for the operation. You're charming and I fell into the plan like the naive mark. I was the dirty little secret, but you had the big one. The four million dollar one. And you chose to keep it from me. Why?"

Again she panned the group with her eyes. "Am I such a threat to you all? Was there some way you could keep the money and never tell me about it? Even when you knew I was going into a room of people baring their teeth for a story, you didn't consider letting me know there was a bomb hidden somewhere that I should be prepared for. You let me find out with microphones in my face, lights blaring in front of me, and cameras rolling. I don't know what kind of people the Claytons were, but they certainly don't seem like the kind who would be proud of what you've all done since I met you."

She paused to take a breath and calm her rapidly beating heart.

"From the beginning I knew there was something wrong about the way you all appeared to accept me. Now I know it was a sham and I never want to see any of you again."

"Stephanie." Owen took a step forward. Her brothers countered with a protective step toward him. Two warring factions ready to blow cannons. Stephanie's head whipped around and pinned Owen with her stare.

"And you." She looked him up and down as if he were a snake. "Don't you come near me again. *Ever.*"

The story hit the evening news and the next morning a picture of her as a three-year-old was printed next to one taken at the press conference on the front page of the *Dallas Herald.* While national news took up the space above the fold, the bottom section was entirely devoted to her. *Kid-*

napped Baby Nets $4 Million Bank Account the head-line read.

Cramped in her small apartment with her uncle and three brothers, Stephanie read none of the accounts. The phone constantly rang and from her bedroom she could hear one or another of her brothers' deep voices as they refused anyone from seeing or talking to her.

Stephanie was grateful for them, her family, people who loved her unconditionally. She knew the truth now. It wasn't she who Owen had been in bed with, in this bed with. It was the four million dollars she was worth that drove him to charm her with his snake dance. Too bad she didn't see the snake in the basket while she was playing the pipe.

Dressed in white shorts and a red striped tank top, she left the sanctity of her bedroom and traversed the small hallway to the main room. There was noise and laughter and it ceased when she walked in.

"Stephanie." Her middle brother, Winston, called her name.

"This is not a wake," she told them. "You're allowed to laugh and have a good time."

"Are you hungry, honey?" Her uncle, who had taken up fat-free cooking after his retirement, was known for trying out new recipes on his family.

"I am," she said, suddenly remembering she hadn't eaten since lunch yesterday.

The phone rang. Stephanie didn't even look at the instrument. Someone answered it and hung up immediately. It was probably a reporter and she wasn't interested in talking to any of them. Stephanie followed her uncle to the kitchen. While discussing meal options, the phone kept ringing. Reaching the point where she couldn't stand it anymore, her brothers found and unplugged all her extensions, washing the apartment in a blessed silence. Thankfully, their cell phones were also quiet.

An hour later, overruled on some tasteless salad involving tofu by three strong men with big appetites and strong shoulders, they sat down to flounder stuffed with crab meat, baked sweet potatoes, green beans, crusty bread and butter and a flowing fountain of sweet iced tea.

No one had mentioned the Claytons since Stephanie came out of her bedroom. The table talk surrounded current events in her brothers lives, how much they liked the way she'd decorated the apartment, as if they hadn't seen it before, and the food.

Stephanie pushed her empty plate away from her. She'd finished the portion she had and wanted no more. She also wanted everyone to stop skating around the subject. Looking them over one by one, she was proud they were her family and prouder that they had rallied for her when she needed them. But that time had passed.

"I want you all to go home," she said.

Forks scraping against dishes ceased moving. Silence dominated the room and four pairs of eyes turned to stare at her.

"What?" her uncle said.

"I mean it. I want you to go home."

"Why?" Logan asked.

"Don't think I don't appreciate you coming. I couldn't have been more pleased when you stepped forward to protect me yesterday. But this is my fight and I have to fight it."

"Stef, they're a powerful family." Only Jared ever called her Stef. "I've done some checking on them and what I've found out tells me they're well connected and can manipulate things to their will."

"I know that. And now that I know the game, I can handle it."

"There will be reporters dogging you for days if you're lucky, weeks if you're not." Her uncle pushed his plate aside. He'd had the tofu salad, but also sneaked a couple of pieces of bread and fish on his plate, too.

"You don't have to worry about me. I'm very resilient."

Uncle Jack stared at her. He recognized her words and knew from where they came. Whenever she had an argument or disagreement with her aunt and her uncle came to console her, she'd tell him she was very resilient. Whenever she didn't perform well in her sport or some school project, she would tell him she was very resilient. And the truth was, she was. She'd been knocked down by Owen and his family, but she would get up and go on. Plenty of people had been in love before and survived it. She would be one of them.

"This time you don't have to be, honey." Her uncle's fatherly voice brought her thoughts back to the table.

"I want to be. I'm not going to play their game. It's not the money that I'm after. I've built my business on customer service, being able to bring to my clients what they envision. I can't stay imprisoned here in my apartment. I have jobs to do, people depending on me. I need to stand up to the bullies and let them know I am not backing away from my responsibilities. And that they can't pull my strings as if I were some puppet."

"What about the money?" Logan whispered.

She dropped her head for a moment. "I don't

know. I haven't decided about that. The account has been there for thirty-four years. It'll wait a little longer."

"I know a good lawyer you can talk to," Winston offered.

"Thanks." She smiled. "Let's hope it doesn't come to that."

"Stef, what are you going to do?"

"I'm going to call the Claytons and set up a meeting with them. This time I won't be so emotional."

"You're not going into that lion's den alone," Jared, the youngest, stated.

"Yes, I am. It's the only way I retain my self-respect. I have to meet them, on their ground. And I'm going to win."

When the phone rang Owen snatched it from the cradle. He hadn't been able to reach Stephanie for two days. Each time he called her one of her brothers hung up. He was ready to go to her apartment and storm though the door, insisting on talking to her. But as it happened when he wanted to do something else, he had a hard time getting out of the office. Staying home wasn't an option. Dean and Rosa were still there and the looks they gave him told him they clearly disapproved of his actions.

"Owen Clayton," he said, controlling his voice with the same iron will he used to keep from squeezing the receiver into a fine powder.

"Mr. Clayton, this is Stephanie Hunter."

He fell back in his chair. All the air left his lungs and his muscles collapsed at the sound of her voice. However, it was very formal. She'd called him *Mr. Clayton.* She'd never done that.

"Stephanie, we need to talk."

"That's why I'm calling. I'd like to meet with you and your family as soon as possible. I hope they're still in town."

"Not all of them. Brad and Mallory had to get back to the hospital in Philly."

"I want to talk to you all at once. Can you hook up that television communication system you mentioned?"

"When?"

"Wednesday night?"

Two days, he thought. "Sure, I can do that."

"Seven o'clock at your house."

"Stephanie, I'd like to see you before then. We need to talk. I need to explain."

There was silence on the phone for a second. She was weighing his request. Owen prayed she'd grant it.

"Wednesday will be enough time. I'll be there at seven."

She hung up.

Owen wanted to pound the phone on his highly polished desk. She hadn't given him a chance to say a word and he couldn't call her back because he knew he'd get one of her brothers and the connection would be cut as quickly as he could dial.

He had to find a way to talk to her. Explain. Tell her he meant her no harm and—more important—that he'd fallen in love with her.

Stephanie drove to Emilie's house. She had to get out of her apartment. The reporters hovering around had made it a prison.

"The deed is done," she said when Emilie opened the door.

Emilie looked behind her, then up and down the street.

"How'd you get here?"

"Without my shadows, you mean?"

Emilie nodded.

"Logan left me his car. He took mine. It's the way I've been able to get in an out of my building. Of course, the sunglasses help." She slipped a pair of pink, plastic and very elaborately carved sunglasses on her face.

"And the wig," Emilie said with a laugh. "Come in before one of my neighbors calls the newspaper. Or the costume police."

Stephanie carried a pizza box and two bottles of wine. She wore a long blonde wig that completely covered her hair and hung down to the middle of her back.

"You stopped for pizza?"

She pulled the glasses off and held them up. "Living dangerously."

"Go in there. I"ll get some glasses." Instead of going to the kitchen, Stephanie went to Emilie's great room, a huge vaulted-ceiling room with skylights and a two-story fireplace, where a DVD of *The Wiz* played on her big-screen television. By the time Emilie joined her, Stephanie had removed the wig and had a slice of pizza in her hand.

"I see you've already started." Emilie looked at the box where two slices were missing.

"It smelled so good in the car I couldn't resist."

When Emilie poured the wine, Stephanie accepted a glass and drank. "I'm going to have to sleep here tonight," she said.

"Why?" Emilie asked, using the remote control to mute the sound on Diana Ross easing on down the road.

"I'm going to drink too much wine."

Emilie laughed. "A planned drunk."

"I deserve it."

Emilie served herself, using a paper plate for the pizza. She folded the tomato pie lengthwise and took a healthy bite. "What did you mean by the deed is done?"

Stephanie ran her tongue over her upper lip as if she were part of a conspiracy. She curled up in her favorite chair, holding her glass of wine.

"I called Owen this afternoon. We're going to meet on Wednesday, some of them by satellite hookup."

"What do you plan to do, come Wednesday?"

"I don't know. I thought of giving them the money back, but that would be insane." She held the wine up to the light, inspecting it, and drank again. "The Claytons set up the fund. Seventeen years ago it would have helped out and it wasn't nearly so much money."

"But it was set up for you."

"They didn't even know if I was alive. They just never took the money out after the kidnapping. They probably hoped someday I would be found."

"And you were," Emilie reminded her. "That day is now. The trust is blind. It doesn't know or care that you're out of college. All it knows is that when the facts are presented to the bank, they match. And you're a woman who needs the money."

"It's more than I need. With that much money I don't need a business. I never have to work again."

"But you would?"

Stephanie nodded. Emilie knew her well. Stephanie also knew Emilie. Neither woman would retire to a life of luxury. Stephanie took pride in her work. She wanted to continue it, building her business exactly as she had before she became the story of the moment.

"You could also do some good with that money, scholarship funds, donations to charities, aid for underprivileged children—"

"Help for adoptive children searching for their birth parents?" Stephanie raised her eyebrows.

"You've thought of these things?"

Stephanie drank and nodded.

"And . . ."

The doorbell rang then. Both women looked at each other. "Are you expecting anyone?" Stephanie asked, stiffening. Doorbells and ringing telephones were not her friends.

Emilie shook her head, getting to her feet. "I wasn't even expecting you. Do you think the reporters followed you?"

"They could have. I'm not a secret agent, but I thought I was pretty crafty at eluding them."

Both women walked from the great room, through the dining room, to come to the center hall from the side. Emilie lived in a center hall colonial that had been built during the recent boom in electronic industries in Texas. When the bottom fell out of the market, she picked up a fantastic brick house on ten acres of land in a quick sale well below market value. The main entrance was a double set of teakwood doors, each containing a huge oval of beveled glass. While the glass was frosted and contained an etched design, anyone on the outside could see the pattern of a figure approaching it. Keeping their steps soft in case reporters were outside, they peered through the side panels.

"It's a man," Emilie whispered. "He's alone."

"It's Owen."

* * *

Emilie opened the door. "Owen Clayton, you must be lost."

"I know she's here, Emilie. I need to talk to her."

"She doesn't want to talk to you."

"Please."

It was that word that got her. *Please.* Stephanie stood in the dining room, out of view, but not out of earshot. Owen sounded desperate. It could be the two glasses of wine she'd drunk, or the way she always reacted to him, but she knew she was going to talk to him.

She stepped out of her hiding place and walked behind Emilie. Owen's face lifted when he saw her.

"It's all right, Emilie. I can talk to him." It seemed childish to hide behind a wall and refuse to talk to someone.

"Come on in." Emilie stepped back, opening the door wide. Owen looked tired, as if he wasn't sleeping well. Stephanie's heart beat a little faster. At least he was having the same experience she was.

They went to the great room. Emilie gathered the wine bottles and glasses and the cold pizza. "Owen, can I get you anything?"

"No, I'm fine."

She looked at Stephanie. "You need some coffee."

"I hate coffee."

"Still," she said. Then turning to Owen. "She commits to nothing tonight. She's had too much wine." Emilie's voice was authoritative, like a mother's.

"I understand."

Looking at Stephanie she said, "I'll be in the kitchen if you need me."

"How did you know I was here?" Stephanie

asked when Emilie left them and they were seated opposite each other. The television was still on although the DVD had ended long ago. The movie logo remained on the screen. Stephanie picked up the remote control and turned the unit off. Her head was a little light and the constant movement on the screen was distracting.

"I followed you," Owen said.

"What is it with you Claytons stalking me?"

Owen sat up straight. Stalking was a crime and he looked as if she were accusing him of such. "You know I wasn't stalking you."

She did. Rosa had followed her the day she had lunch at the Margharita House and now Owen.

"I saw you leave the garage driving your brother's car. I thought it was a good ploy and since none of the reporters noticed that you'd switched or wore that wig, I left at the same time."

"You said you wanted to talk to me. About what?"

"About everything, us, my family, the money."

"We're having a meeting on Wednesday."

"I couldn't wait that long. And for once I don't want my family involved."

Stephanie watched him. He looked nervous. She'd never seen him that way before. Owen Clayton was always so sure of himself. He exuded confidence. He walked and talked as if he knew where he was going, how to get there and explain his every motivation to anyone who wanted to listen. This Owen was different, more vulnerable, more human.

"Coming in," Emilie announced. She carried a tray with coffee, cups, milk, and sweeteners. Owen immediately stood up and took it. He placed it on the low table where the pizza and wine had been.

Stephanie's cup was already made. She took it and sipped the hot liquid, making a face at the taste.

"Drink it all," Emilie ordered as she left them.

"Why didn't you tell me about the money?" Stephanie went for the question that meant the most to her.

"I'm not sure. I thought I had a reason, but the more I got to know you the less sense it made."

"What was the reason?"

"I thought you were a gold digger." Stephanie's eyes opened wide and she stared at him. "At least that's the reason I told myself."

"Why would you think that?"

"You pointed out how you needed money for your business and your appearance at the point when my mother died just seemed too coincidental."

"But I explained that."

"I know and I believed you."

"So when you discovered I wasn't after the money, why did you keep it a secret?"

"It was never our intention to keep the money from you. We couldn't if we wanted to. The account is in your name and my parents'. As soon as the story on you hit the papers, Mr. Frankel of Frankel, Williams and Williams, the law firm handling the account, called me and asked if I knew how to reach you. I gave them your address and phone number, but your brothers kept hanging up on him."

"I told them I wanted no calls. We had to unplug the phones to keep them from ringing."

"I'm sorry. All this is my fault. If I'd only told you when I found out you were Cynthia Clayton. But by then I was in love with you."

Stephanie's cup rattled. Her throat closed off

and she put her hand over the top of the hot liquid to keep it steady. Owen moved from his seat to the sofa where she sat. He took the coffee cup and set it on the table.

"It got so complicated. Every time I'd see you, you'd push me away, say you only wanted a business relationship. I'd never felt about a woman the way I feel about you. It scared me to death."

"Yet you found a way to step around my objections."

"You left me no choice. But back to the money. I thought if I told you about it, you might leave or you might think I was only interested in you because I knew about it."

That hadn't occurred to her. But what if it were true?

"Don't do that," Owen said.

"Do what?"

"Don't start to second guess my motives. They were honest and true. Don't think that our time together, that what we found in each other has anything to do with the money. It doesn't. Believe me. It doesn't."

She searched his features. Her brain wasn't completely clear, but his voice was sincere and his eyes implored her to find the genuineness in his voice. She believed him.

"I'm in love with you. I think I've been in love with you since we talked about old movies at the Women's Museum."

"You never invited me to watch one with you."

"When we were together we never found the time." He smiled and Stephanie returned it. She knew he was remembering their times together, their frantic lovemaking and the heights to which they could reach when wreathed around each other like a never-ending circle.

"The night after the dinner at my house, the family decided we should tell you. We wanted to get together and tell you as a group, so there would be no misunderstanding."

"But the story hit the papers and the word was out."

"If I'd known it would come out there, I'd never have let you go in that room without the knowledge. One of the reasons the entire family was there for the press conference was to also tell you about the account. We'd planned to take you back to the house and tell you all about it."

When he finished the room was too quiet. Circumstances had gotten out of control and their plans had been waylaid.

"I came here tonight to ask you to forgive me. Will you?"

Stephanie believed him. She saw the truth in his eyes. "Of course I forgive you."

Owen moved quickly, gathered her in his arms and kissed her. Stephanie's heart was hammering in her ears and her body began its usual meltdown. Warmed by two glasses of wine the meltdown wouldn't take long. She'd missed him, missed being close, smelling his aftershave and knowing the feel of his arms holding her close.

Owen leaned back and looked down at her. "I have one more question to ask you."

Stephanie waited. She didn't know what to expect. She'd already forgiven Owen. What else was there? "Ask," she said.

"Will you marry me?"

Stephanie was stunned. Owen Clayton, playboy, Casanova, can't be tied down by one woman, had just asked her to marry him. She didn't know what to say.

"Emilie said I couldn't commit to anything tonight."

"Not to that question," Emilie shouted from the other room. "That one you can answer."

They turned at the sound of her voice, looking toward the kitchen. They couldn't see her, but turned back to each other and laughed. "Well?" Owen asked.

"Yes." Tears glistened in her eyes. "Yes, Owen Clayton. Yes, I'll marry you."

Wednesday night arrived. An attempted bank robbery and afternoon hostile situation sent the reporters camped outside of Stephanie's building scrambling for a bigger prize than her thirty-four-year old news. Owen picked her up at the front door and drove her to his house.

One room housing a television and an elaborate array of equipment was set up and waiting. An L-shaped sofa faced the big screen. Stephanie sat on the long side. Owen took the seat next to her. Rosa and Dean came in carrying trays of cold cuts, vegetables, and cheeses. Rosa handed her a drink and sat on the short side. Dean fiddled with the controls and suddenly Clayton family members began to appear on the screen in small boxes. He backed up, sitting next to his sister.

When Mariette Randall appeared on the screen, Stephanie relaxed a bit. The older woman smiled at Stephanie and she knew she had at least one true friend in the matrix of faces.

"Hello, everyone." Stephanie felt foolish speaking to the television. A chorus of hi's, and hello's came back and she relaxed a bit. Owen took her hand and nothing mattered after that.

"Since I called this meeting," Stephanie said. "I

should begin." She smiled at them all, not in the least intimidated as she had been the first time she had them all in one place staring at her. "At the time my reasons were very different."

She looked at Owen. He winked at her, his eyes full of love. Then he looked at the screen.

"Owen?" Rosa questioned. She'd obviously seen the look that passed between them.

"We called you all here for an announcement."

Stephanie held her hand up. A huge diamond engagement ring sparkled from the third finger of her left hand. "I'm really going to be a Clayton," she said.

Rosa was on her feet in seconds. "Why didn't you tell me?" she said, hugging Stephanie and then her brother. Noise came from the screens. It was unintelligible. Stephanie could hear none of it.

After a moment Dean tried to restore order. Lifting his glass, containing orange juice, he toasted the happy couple. Stephanie had tears in her eyes that matched those in Rosa's.

"Have you set a date yet?"

"No," Stephanie said. "We only got engaged yesterday."

"But we will soon," Owen interjected.

"Are you going to be my new aunt?" a little girl asked.

"Hi, Sam," Owen said. "This is Stephanie and yes, she's going to be your new aunt."

"Can I be in the wedding?"

They all laughed. After a few more questions and more congratulations, everyone settled down.

"Owen and I spent a lot of time talking yesterday. He explained all about finding me, discovering the money and the dilemma you had in telling me about it."

Owen squeezed her hand and slipped his arm around her waist. "It wasn't all your fault. I wasn't the model friend and my methods of finding out about you wasn't done in an open and direct manner. I hope we can put it all behind us and be a real family."

"I'm sure we can," Brad said.

There were smiles and nods all around. Moments later the screens began to blank out as they all hung up.

"We should give you guys some time, too." Dean said. "Rosa and I are going to a movie."

He took Rosa's hand and pulled her out of the room.

"Why do I think that was planned?" she asked Owen.

"They're just being polite."

"Ah, and what are we going to do?"

"How about we watch an old movie?"

Stephanie leaned over and kissed Owen. His arms came around her and dragged her onto his lap, where his mouth began the sorcery that always happened between them.

One day, she thought, they would get around to seeing a movie together.

But not today.

Epilogue

The crowd that spanned the small patch of earth around Devon and Reuben Clayton's graves was smaller than it had been a year ago. Today there was only family, extended family, and a few friends. The Claytons had opened their arms to the Hunters and the Carters and all had joined together. With the exception of Aunt Meriweather everyone was in attendance. Mariette, without a hat or covering to hide her face, stood on one side of Stephanie. Owen occupied the space on the other.

The minister performed a short ceremony and unveiled the stone baring Devon's name. Made of pink marble, the headstone had deeply carved letters. *Devon Clayton,* it proclaimed. *Beloved Wife and Mother. We Miss You.*

Stephanie held a single red rose. Separating from the family she placed it atop the marker.

"She would be proud of you, Stephanie," Luanne said. "What you're doing is something I know she would have done."

"She would be proud of all of us," Stephanie answered. "Neither one of the Clayton parents could have asked for a better family."

Returning to the group, Stephanie slipped her arm around Owen. For several moments all eyes were on the place marking the life of Devon Clayton. Stephanie thought it was a remarkable life.

The red rose hung across the top. Stephanie wasn't feeling what the other Claytons felt about their mother. She was grateful to her and to the biological father she had never met. They'd left her a legacy that she hoped would change lives for the better. They hadn't intended it for the purpose she was using it, but she knew they would approve.

Owen must have felt her confusion. "What is it?" he asked.

"Nothing, really. I was just thinking about the money they left me."

"They'd think your decision is the best use of it," Owen reinforced.

"I'm not using it all," Stephanie said. "I am putting some into my business."

"But the bulk you're using to help other adoptees find their birth parents," Brad stated.

"It's exactly the kind of thing they would have done." Luanne's voice was reverent when she spoke.

"And they'd be overjoyed that finally you'd been brought home," Dean said.

Owen tightened his arm around her waist. Stephanie stared at the pink headstone. Silently she said thank you to her mother. Stephanie was engaged to Owen Clayton. She'd never been happier in her life. Without Devon's last request to Owen to find Cynthia their lives would have taken different paths and she would have never found the family that loved her.

Or the man by her side who could never make up for her past, but could provide her with a future happiness that no one else in the world could.

Dear Reader,

Many of you have been asking when I was going to write Owen's story. Finally it's here. I hope you enjoyed *The Secret*.

This story is near and dear to my heart. The Clayton children were all adopted and found better lives as they grew into adulthood. I'm adopting for the second time and recently I attended a picnic for foster and adoptive children. There must have been 3,000 people at this park. I was amazed there were so many people who opened their hearts and homes to children in need. I wanted to personally hug every one of them and say thank you for making the world a better place.

The Claytons are these kind of people. They have big hearts and a love for each other even though their family came together by the efforts of a loving couple's tragedy and the children's circumstance. I believe Stephanie says it best when describing her own less than perfect fate: "... *without those loving parents to guide and love them, this family, who are only together by happenstance, might be far different today.*

Take a moment out of your busy day to hug a child. It doesn't matter if it's your child, a neighbor's or one you meet in the mall. Let someone know that you care. Random acts of kindness work.

I'm busy working on my next novel, but if you'd like to hear more about *The Secret*, and other books

I've written or upcoming releases, please send a business-size, self-addressed, stamped envelope to me at the following address:

Shirley Hailstock
P.O. Box 513
Plainsboro, NJ 08536

You can also visit my Web page at: http://www.geocities.com/shailstock.

Sincerely yours,

Shirley Hailstock